THE **AWESOME** ADVENTURE

DINOSAUR COVE™

DINOSAUR COVE™

THE **AWESOME** ADVENTURE

by
REX STONE

3 BOOKS IN 1

illustrated by
MIKE SPOOR

Series created by
Working Partners Ltd

OXFORD
UNIVERSITY PRESS

OXFORD
UNIVERSITY PRESS

Great Clarendon Street, Oxford OX2 6DP
Oxford University Press is a department of the University of Oxford.
It furthers the University's objective of excellence in research, scholarship,
and education by publishing worldwide in

Oxford   New York

Auckland   Cape Town   Dar es Salaam   Hong Kong   Karachi
Kuala Lumpur   Madrid   Melbourne   Mexico City   Nairobi
New Delhi   Shanghai   Taipei   Toronto

With offices in

Argentina   Austria   Brazil   Chile   Czech Republic   France   Greece
Guatemala   Hungary   Italy   Japan   Poland   Portugal   Singapore
South Korea   Switzerland   Thailand   Turkey   Ukraine   Vietnam

Oxford is a registered trade mark of Oxford University Press
in the UK and in certain other countries

British Library Cataloguing in Publication Data

Data available

ISBN: 978-0-19-278991-4

1 3 5 7 9 10 8 6 4 2

Printed in Great Britain
Paper used in the production of this book is a natural,
recyclable product made from wood grown in sustainable forests
The manufacturing process conforms to the environmental
regulations of the country of origin

CONTENTS

DINOSAUR COVE™

FLIGHT OF THE WINGED SERPENT

by
REX STONE

illustrated by
MIKE SPOOR

Series created by
Working Partners Ltd

OXFORD
UNIVERSITY PRESS

Special thanks to Jan Burchett and Sara Vogler

Especially for Theo and Ben Wheadon, with love

FACT FILE

▷ JAMIE HAS JUST MOVED FROM THE CITY TO LIVE IN THE LIGHTHOUSE IN DINOSAUR COVE. JAMIE'S DAD IS OPENING A DINOSAUR MUSEUM ON THE BOTTOM FLOOR OF THE LIGHTHOUSE. WHEN JAMIE GOES HUNTING FOR FOSSILS IN THE CRUMBLING CLIFFS ON THE BEACH HE MEETS A LOCAL BOY, TOM, AND THE TWO DISCOVER AN AMAZING SECRET: A WORLD WITH REAL, LIVE DINOSAURS! WALKING ON THE GROUND WITH THE DINOSAURS IS ONE THING, BUT FLYING IN THE AIR WITH THEM IS A DIFFERENT MATTER!

JAMIE

- **FULL NAME:** JAMIE MORGAN
- **AGE:** 8 YEARS
- **SIZE:** 1 JATOM*
- **TOP SPEED:** 10 KPH
- **LIKES:** FOSSIL HUNTING AND LEARNING ABOUT DINOSAURS
- **DISLIKES:** BEING STUCK INDOORS

Jamie's eye

Jamie's foot

Jamie's hand

*NOTE: A JATOM IS THE SIZE OF JAMIE OR TOM: 125 CM TALL AND 27 KG IN WEIGHT

TOM

- **FULL NAME:** THOMAS CLAY
- **AGE:** 8 YEARS
- **SIZE:** 1 JATOM*
- **TOP SPEED:** 10 KPH
- **LIKES:** TRACKING ANIMALS AND EXPLORING WILDLIFE
- **DISLIKES:** RAINY DAYS

Tom's eye   Tom's hand

WANNA

- **FULL NAME:** WANNANOSAURUS
- **AGE:** 65 – 80 MILLION YEARS**
- **SIZE:** LESS THAN A JATOM*
- **TOP SPEED:** 50 KPH, ESPECIALLY WHEN BEING CHASED BY A T-REX
- **LIKES:** STINKY GINGKO FRUIT AND BANGING HIS HEAD ON TREE TRUNKS
- **DISLIKES:** SCARY DINOSAURS

Wanna's head   Wanna's foot

*NOTE: A JATOM IS THE SIZE OF JAMIE OR TOM: 125 CM TALL AND 27 KG IN WEIGHT
**NOTE: SCIENTISTS CALL THIS PERIOD THE LATE CRETACEOUS

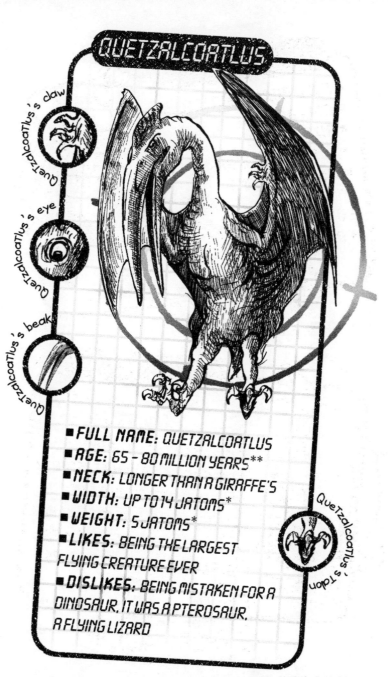

QUETZALCOATLUS

Quetzalcoatlus's claw

Quetzalcoatlus's eye

Quetzalcoatlus's beak

Quetzalcoatlus's talon

- **FULL NAME:** QUETZALCOATLUS
- **AGE:** 65 – 80 MILLION YEARS**
- **NECK:** LONGER THAN A GIRAFFE'S
- **WIDTH:** UP TO 14 JATOMS*
- **WEIGHT:** 5 JATOMS*
- **LIKES:** BEING THE LARGEST FLYING CREATURE EVER
- **DISLIKES:** BEING MISTAKEN FOR A DINOSAUR. IT WAS A PTEROSAUR, A FLYING LIZARD

*NOTE: A JATOM IS THE SIZE OF JAMIE OR TOM: 125 CM TALL AND 27 KG IN WEIGHT
**NOTE: SCIENTISTS CALL THIS PERIOD THE LATE CRETACEOUS

DINOSAUR COVE

Village

Marina

Sealight Head

12

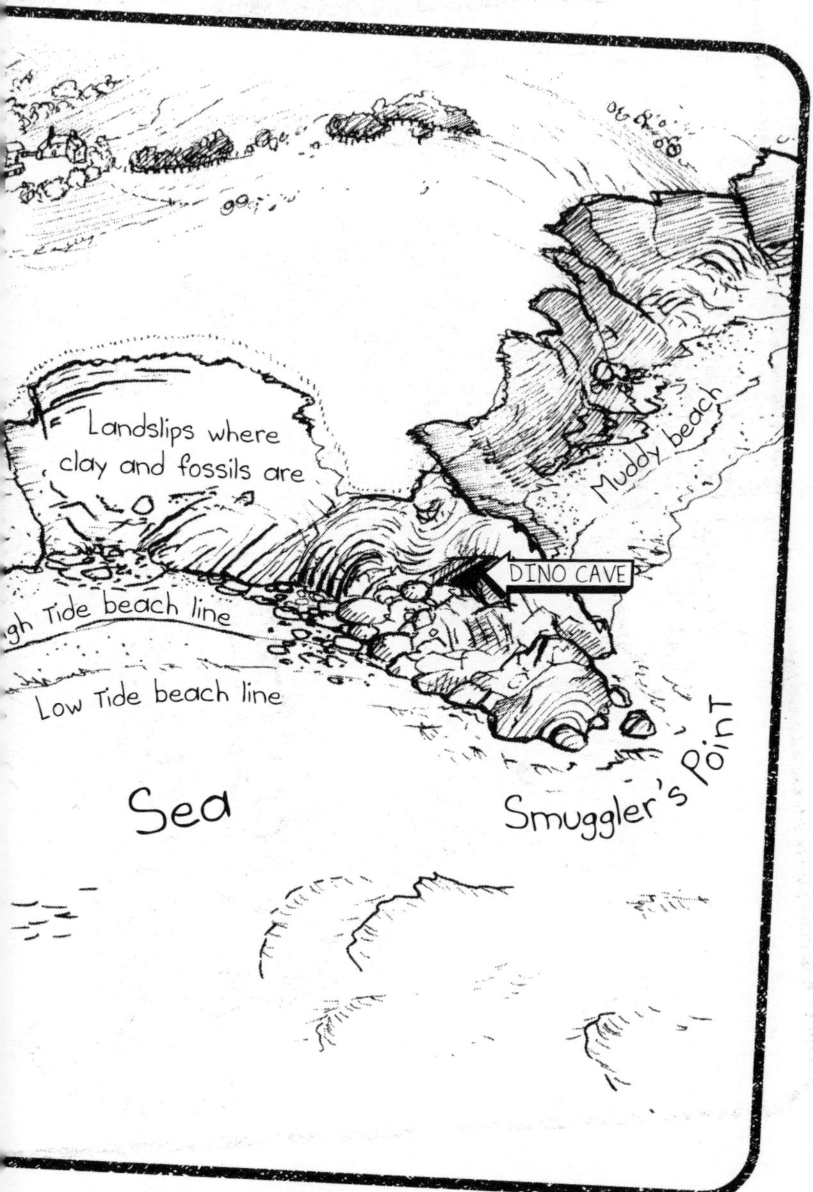

Landslips where
clay and fossils are

Muddy beach

DINO CAVE

gh Tide beach line

Low Tide beach line

Sea

Smuggler's Point

CHAPTER 1

'This exhibit looks so cool!' exclaimed Jamie, as his best friend Tom glued on the last miniature jungle tree.

The two boys had spent the morning painting the prehistoric landscape and were just finishing the scenery. The scale model was as big as the table top and was going to be one of the exhibits in Jamie's dad's new dinosaur museum on the bottom floor of the old lighthouse where they lived.

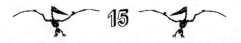

'The marsh is my favourite,' Tom said, putting down the glue.

The model was labelled 'Late Cretaceous Period' and had a jungle, a plain, a beach with cliffs, and an eerie-looking marsh. Dad had set up a smoke machine under the table so that smoke blew over the marsh like mist.

Dad walked into the room with the post. 'You two have done a brilliant job painting the ocean,' he told them, and grinned at their paint-splattered clothes. 'And yourselves!'

Next, Jamie and Tom added the most
important items to the display—the
dinosaurs! They arranged a herd of triceratops
on the green plain.

'They're just right there,' said Dad. 'They
look as if they're grazing.' He stuck his head
into a crate and started rummaging. Sawdust
flew everywhere. 'Can't find the
edmontosaurus,' came his muffled voice.
'I'm sure they're in here somewhere.'

'Dad's models are great,' whispered
Jamie, 'but they're not as good
as the real thing.'

Jamie and Tom had a secret. They had discovered the entrance to an amazing land of living dinosaurs, and they visited it whenever they could.

Jamie picked up a Tyrannosaurus Rex and made it run across the plain towards an ankylosaurus with a roar.

Tom snatched up the ankylosaurus. 'Not such an easy meal, you bully!' He swung the tiny anky's clubbed tail at the T-Rex.

'Whoops!' Tom gasped as the T-Rex went flying out of Jamie's hand towards a shelf full of model creatures.

WHACK!

The T-Rex crashed into a large winged creature which wobbled and fell. Jamie dived like a goalie and caught it before it hit the floor.

'Good catch!' gasped Tom.

Jamie's dad came running over.

'Sorry, Mr Morgan,' said Tom. 'Is it broken?'

Jamie's dad checked the model's wings. 'No damage done,' he told them. 'Now, where should this go on the display?'

Jamie looked at the long beak, the outstretched wings, and bony crest on the head. 'It's a sort of pterosaur, isn't it?'

'Yes, it's a quetzalcoatlus. Here's its label.'

'*Ket-sal-kow-at-lus*,' Jamie read. 'That's a mouthful.'

'The biggest flying reptile of them all,' Dad explained. 'It had a twelve metre wingspan.'

'That's more than six Dads lying head to toe.' Jamie flung his arms out wide.

'What a monster!' Tom said.

'One thing we don't know

is where these quetzies nested,' said Dad.
'On the marsh, on the beach, or in the
jungle.' He put the quetzy back on the shelf.
'Here's a quest for you, boys. Do some
research and help me decide where on the
model to put it. That'll keep you out of
trouble.'

Jamie and Tom grinned at each other.
They knew exactly where to find out where
the quetzalcoatlus nested—Dino World!

Jamie scooped up his backpack and charged
after Tom down the rocky steps from the
lighthouse. They raced across the

pebbly beach, whooping with
excitement, to the steep
headland path. Clambering
over the mossy boulders they were
soon at the old smugglers' cave—and the
entrance to their secret world.

Tom slipped inside with
Jamie close behind. They
squeezed through the tiny
opening to the second chamber.
Jamie shone his torch over the
rock floor.

'Here are the footprints,' he said. 'Let's go!'

One step at a time, Jamie and Tom followed the fossilized dinosaur tracks that led to the wall at the back of the cave. One . . . two . . . The familiar crack of light appeared in the wall . . . three . . . four . . . The crack widened . . . Five!

When Jamie opened his eyes, the ground was spongy under his feet. Jamie and Tom were in Dino World again!

Jamie stepped out of the cave and squinted in the bright sunlight. He breathed in the hot, damp air. 'Awesome!'

A bristly tongue licked his hand. A little dinosaur with greenish brown markings stood looking up hopefully at him.

'It's Wanna!' he cried.

Tom gave the wannanosaurus a welcoming pat on his hard, flat head. Wanna wagged his tail happily and stuck out his tongue to investigate a blue spot on Jamie's shorts.

Grunk! Wanna spat.

'Paint tastes horrible, doesn't it, Wanna?' said Jamie. 'Let's find you some nice, stinky gingkoes to make it better.'

He reached up and picked a handful of sticky orange fruits from a nearby gingko tree.

Wanna gulped down the gingkoes in one go, juice spilling out of his mouth and down his chest. His long, bristly tongue licked his face and he grunked happily.

Jamie stuck a few more gingkoes in his
backpack.

The boys went to the edge of the steep
slope that led down to the jungle. They
scanned the thick green canopy of trees below.

'One thing's for sure,' said Tom, 'quetzies
couldn't live in there—not with that huge
wingspan. The trees are too close together.
And I don't see any nests in the tree tops.'

Jamie opened his Fossil Finder and put
quetzalcoatlus in the search.

'*THOUGHT TO HAVE EATEN LIKE HERON,
DIVING DOWN FOR FISH,*'
he read. 'So maybe
they live near water.'

'Misty Lagoon?' said Tom. 'But I only remember seeing smaller pterosaurs there—nothing as big as a quetzy.'

'How about White Ocean?' said Jamie eagerly. He shielded his eyes with his hand and peered out over the jungle, to where the ocean waves broke in a white line.

Tom whipped his compass out of his pocket. 'West it is.'

The boys made their way down into the thick, damp undergrowth of the jungle. Wanna ran happily alongside them. He stopped to headbutt a pine tree and greedily ate the cones that fell. The shower of cones disturbed a host of brightly coloured butterflies as big as the boys' hands. They swarmed for a moment and then settled on a bush covered in white flowers.

The boys crossed the river and gradually the dense jungle thinned. They passed the lagoon and the ground became sandy, with tall, spiky plants shooting up in places.

'I can hear waves breaking,' exclaimed Tom. 'Race you!'

They charged through the last few trees and out into the sunlight.

'Wow!' breathed Jamie, skidding to a halt. He pointed down the beach. 'Check out those cliffs. They're even higher than back in Dinosaur Cove.'

Sharp ledges and leafy green bushes covered the huge cliff-face. In front of

29

them, the golden beach stretched towards the water. Wanna sniffed around, getting his snout covered in sand.

'Maybe this is his first trip to the seaside.' Jamie laughed. 'Sorry we forgot the bucket and spade, Wanna.'

'Awesome!' shouted Tom above the sound of the crashing breakers and the gusting wind. 'Look at those waves. Fantastic for surfing.'

'If you don't mind the predators,' Jamie

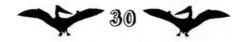

reminded him. 'I bet it's not just lobsters and crabs under there.' He typed *LATE CRETACEOUS SEA CREATURES* into the Fossil Finder and scrolled down the entries.

'*ELASMOSAURUS: HUGE, LONG-NECKED, MARINE REPTILE.*

Looks like the Loch
Ness Monster.' He showed
Tom the picture on the
screen. 'PLATECARPUS: SHARP-
TOOTHED SEA LIZARD. There are sharks, too.'

'I could do a great TV commentary from
my surfboard.' Tom pretended to be riding the
waves and speaking into a microphone.
'Here we have the gigantic platecarpus.
I can see every one of this sea lizard's jagged
teeth and . . . Aaaaagh, it's got me!'

Jamie laughed as his friend fell on the
sand and fought an
invisible platecarpus.

Suddenly Tom jumped to his feet. 'What's that?' He pointed out to the horizon. 'It's the size of a plane.'

Jamie screened his eyes with his hand. Far away over the sea, a huge winged creature was gliding in large graceful circles, rising and falling with the air currents.

Tom whistled. 'It's just like your dad's model. And look, here come some more.'

The two boys looked at each other.

'It's a quetzalcoatlus!' they shouted.

CHAPTER 3

Jamie and Tom watched as the huge quetzies made lazy circles above the surf. One of them was getting closer.

'It's searching for fish,' said Tom. 'Do you think its nest is nearby?'

'It might be in the sand,' suggested Jamie. 'Like a turtle's.'

They walked along the high tide line, crunching through fragments of patterned baculite shell, but couldn't see any imprints or patterns in the ground to suggest a nest.

'Wouldn't this look good in your dad's museum?' Tom said, picking up a shell. 'Shame it would just turn to dust if we took it back.'

'Even if we could,' added Jamie, 'these have been extinct for millions of years. Dad would want to know how we found one that's not a fossil.'

Wanna trotted down the beach and looked suspiciously at the waves.

'Going for a paddle, Wanna?' called Tom.

The little dinosaur crept towards the edge of the water and stuck in his snout.

Grunk!

He spluttered and darted back. The boys burst out laughing.

'The salt must taste worse than paint,' said Jamie. 'Poor Wanna.'

Wanna scratched at his mouth with his front claws as if he was trying to get rid of the taste.

Then Tom spotted a cave at the bottom of the cliffs. 'That would be a great hiding place for the quetzy's nest.'

The boys went to investigate. Jamie pulled out his torch and shone it into the dark beyond the cave entrance but it was empty. There was no sign of a quetzy nest.

AAAARK!

The boys whirled round at the deafening

sound behind them. An enormous shadow was moving over the sand. They dived into the cave mouth. Wanna grunked in alarm and followed.

A gigantic creature swept down and landed on the sand with a loud flapping of wings that sounded like boat sails in the wind. Jamie and Tom stared in amazement. In front of them were two long scaly legs with massive clawed feet. As they looked up they could see a featherless body and neck that seemed to snake up to the sky. It stood above them, as tall as a house, twisting its long neck slowly this way and that. Then it opened its beak and gave out a loud *AAAARK!*

'It's the quetzy,' breathed Tom.

'That's one weird reptile,' said Jamie in amazement. 'Like a fold-up paper aeroplane with skin for wings.'

The huge pterosaur began to clump awkwardly across the sand, head forward,

using the claws on its wings as front feet.

'Bats walk like that,' said Tom. 'I've seen it on a wildlife programme.'

A gust of wind buffeted the quetzy. It ran a few steps on its long skinny legs, caught the updraught and took off.

'See where it goes!' cried Jamie.

The boys dashed out from the shelter of the cave mouth and watched the quetzalcoatlus rise. The wind buffeted it back towards the cliffs, but soon it turned and soared, flapping its powerful wings to gain height. It circled around the cliff top and descended, feet out for landing. At last, with a loud *AAARK*, it disappeared from view.

'I bet its nest is up *there*,' said Jamie. 'We have to get to the top.'

'It'll be a tough climb,' said Tom, squinting up at the cliff-face. 'But we can do it. There are indents for our feet.'

'And we can use
the bushes to cling to,'
agreed Jamie.

SQUAWK!

Something landed on
the sand behind them.
It lay on its back with its
skinny feet in the air.
It looked like a large,
featherless chicken.

'Where did that come
from?' exclaimed Tom,
staring up at the cliffs.

'I don't know,' gasped Jamie.
'Watch out!'

They darted back as a
second one fell out of the sky
and plopped down on to the
sand. 'They must be coming from
up there,' Tom said.

A third creature appeared over
the top of the cliffs. It flapped its
wings desperately and then cartwheeled
down, squawking, to land right in front
of them.

'They've got crests.' Tom pointed to the
little bony lump on top of each head. 'Long
beaks, claws on their wings . . . '

'They're baby quetzies!'

The boys watched as the three young
reptiles struggled to their feet and waddled up
and down flapping their wings.

'They're trying to take off,' said Tom.

'They look like big wind-up toys.' Jamie
grinned at the funny sight.

Grunk, grunk!

Wanna scuttled up to the gawky creatures.
The baby quetzies peered down at him and
squawked happily. 'What is it, boy?' asked
Jamie. 'Are you saying hello?'

Grunk!

Wanna nudged the nearest chick with his nose, then darted out of reach. The little quetzies clumped after him on all fours, squeaking with delight. Wanna stopped, waggled his tail at them and dashed off down the beach. His new playmates followed.

Tom chuckled. 'They're playing tag. Let's get a closer look.'

As soon as they saw the boys coming, the baby quetzies left Wanna and waddled towards them.

'They're not scared of us,' said Tom. 'They look really friendly.'

'Whoa!' Jamie backed off as a long pointed beak was pushed in his face, and another pecked at his trainers. 'A bit too friendly.'

AARK! The boys looked up. The mother quetzy was gliding in circles, looking down angrily, blocking out the sun.

'Run!' shouted Jamie.

Jamie and Tom flattened themselves against the cliff-face, but Wanna hadn't noticed the danger. He ran round the babies, grunking and nudging them to play again.

'Wanna's in danger,' said Tom. 'The mother might attack him!'

'Come here, Wanna,' Jamie shouted but the little quetzies were making so much noise that Wanna didn't hear him.

AAARK!

The huge quetzalcoatlus began to descend, stretching out long, sharp claws as she came.

'We've got to save Wanna!' yelled Jamie, darting forwards.

'It's too late.' Tom pulled his friend back. 'There's nothing we can do.'

Swoosh! The boys felt the rush of air as the giant pterosaur swooped down over the sand. A second later she was making for the sky.

The babies were gone—and so was Wanna!

CHAPTER 4

Jamie and Tom stared open-mouthed as the quetzalcoatlus rose in the air. Wanna and the three chicks were dangling from her claws. They could see the little dinosaur's tail waggling with fright.

Jamie shook Tom's arm. 'We've got to get up those cliffs,' he urged. 'We must rescue Wanna.'

'Too right,' said Tom. 'Before he's turned into quetzy food!'

They began to climb, side by side. It was a slow job. The cliff footholds were very small

and the pale rock crumbled under
their trainers and showered down.
Gradually they edged their way up.

'What's that?' Jamie asked, looking at
something jutting out above them.

'Looks like a ledge of rock,' Tom said.
'It sticks out quite far. And we've got to get
over it. '

Luckily the ledge was covered in creepers.

Jamie gave one a tug. It held firm. 'There's
only one thing for it,' he said.

'OK, boss,' grinned Tom.

Gripping tightly with his hands and
hooking his feet over the creepers, Jamie
hung upside down underneath the ledge.
He made his way like a spider on a
ceiling to the edge of the overhang.

He scrabbled with his fingers to find a handhold on the top of the ledge. Suddenly he lost his grip and found himself hanging by his trainers. It was like dangling from a giant climbing frame—a climbing frame with a deadly drop beneath it.

'Jamie!' yelled Tom in alarm.

'I'm OK,' Jamie shouted back. He swung his arms up as hard as he could and on the third attempt managed to grab the foliage again. He waited until he'd got his breath back, then, tensing every muscle, he heaved himself onto the top of the ledge.

Soon Tom's hand appeared. Jamie took

 51

him firmly by the wrist and helped him up.
The boys saw that the top of the ledge was
also covered by a spongy bed of creepers.

'Awesome!' breathed Tom. 'We did it.'

'And there's the top of the cliffs,' cried
Jamie, pointing a little way above their heads.
'Wanna, here we come!'

They scrambled up to the cliff edge and
looked over. It was nothing like the cliffs back
home, which were covered in grass and wild
flowers. Here there was bare rock with a few
scattered prickly plants sticking up.

The mother quetzy sat a little way from them.

'There's no sign of Wanna,' said Jamie, 'or the babies.'

'Let's get behind that bush with the red flowers,' whispered Tom. 'The quetzy won't be able to see us there.'

Jamie and Tom crawled commando style to the thick bush. Jamie carefully parted some leaves. The mother quetzy filled his view.

'The nest must be somewhere close by,'
he told Tom. 'But it's hard to spot it with that
huge pterosaur in the way.'

'Ask her to move,' grinned Tom.

'*You* ask her!'

As if she had heard, the mother quetzy
waddled to the cliff edge, folded its wings and
raised its head, gazing out to sea.

'Look at the three bony crests over there,'
whispered Jamie. 'Those are the babies. The
mother must be guarding them in their nest.'

The baby quetzies were sitting in a hollow
a few metres away.

'But where's Wanna?' Tom grabbed Jamie's arm. 'What if we're too late and they've already had him for dinner?'

Grunk, grunk!

A cone-shaped leathery hat with two brown eyes under it appeared over the edge of the nest.

'There he is!' exclaimed Tom.

'He's OK,' breathed Jamie in relief. 'But what's he wearing?'

'It's one of the quetzy eggshells,' Tom giggled. He stuck a hand out of the bush. 'Here, Wanna,' he beckoned.

'Come on, Wanna,' Jamie tried to coax him.

But Wanna just stared at them. He seemed comfortable with his new friends.

'How do we lure him out?' said Tom.

Jamie rummaged in his backpack. 'I'll offer him a gingko. That should bring him running.'

Trying to keep out of sight of the mother, Jamie crawled towards the nest. He had reached the edge when she spotted him.

AAARK!
Jamie ducked as
the huge wing nearly
caught him. He darted
back to the bushes and Tom
pulled him between the leaves and out of
sight. The gingko was squashed in his hand.

'It's just like on the documentaries,' said
Tom. 'The mother is protecting her young
and that makes her very dangerous.'

'One whack and I'd have been over the
edge,' puffed Jamie. 'Now what?'

Tom didn't answer. He was looking up.

Another quetzy was circling the nest.

'That one's even bigger than this one,' he said. 'It could be the dad.'

AARK, AAARK!

The male quetzy landed next to the nest. His cry was deep and rumbling. The babies greeted him with screeches and squeals. Their heads bobbed and they eagerly opened their beaks. Wanna sat looking puzzled under his leathery hat. The dad bent his head down in a sudden motion and opened his mouth wide— right over Wanna's head. The boys heard a strange gurgling noise from his throat.

'He's going to eat him!' Jamie gasped. 'We've got to do something.'

But the male quetzy moved his head away from Wanna and over one of his babies. He made the strange gurgling sound again and suddenly was sick into the baby quetzy's

open beak. The little chick gulped hungrily. Then the dad bent to the next chick and puked again. The chick opened its mouth, caught the goo and gulped hungrily.

'Gross!' said Jamie.

'It's just like birds feeding their young,' said Tom. 'They mash down the food in their own throats and then bring it back up for them. And it's Wanna's turn now.'

The father gurgled again and all at once Wanna and his eggshell hat were covered in steaming yellow goo. Wanna looked surprised.

Jamie laughed. 'They think he's one of their chicks!'

Wanna shook his head, splattering yellow goo everywhere. His eggshell hat went flying. Then he clambered out of the nest and began to sniff and scuff at the ground.

'That's our Wanna,' whispered Tom. 'He never sits still for long. He's too nosy.'

'I'd get out if a dinosaur was sick on my head,' said Jamie.

Tom craned round the bush. 'Wanna,' he called softly. 'Here, boy.'

AAARK!

The mother quetzy had seen
Wanna. Wriggling her wings
irritably, she scuttled round the
nest and nudged him back
with her beak.

When the father had finished feeding all
the chicks, he took off and soared away.

'This is our best chance to get Wanna,'
said Jamie. 'I'd rather face one fierce quetzy
than two.'

'Agreed,' Tom nodded.

The chicks began to squawk excitedly as
the mother picked one of them up in her beak
and plonked it down at the cliff edge.

'What's she doing?' Jamie gasped.
'The baby's going to fall off again.'

The little quetzy
teetered on the edge
for a moment and
suddenly leapt off.
They just had time
to see it flapping its
wings frantically before it
plummeted out of sight.
The mother didn't seem
to mind. She nudged
another chick out of the
nest and pushed it to
the drop. This one
flapped its wings and
actually flew for a few
seconds before it
plunged down.
They could hear
its happy squawks
as it fell.

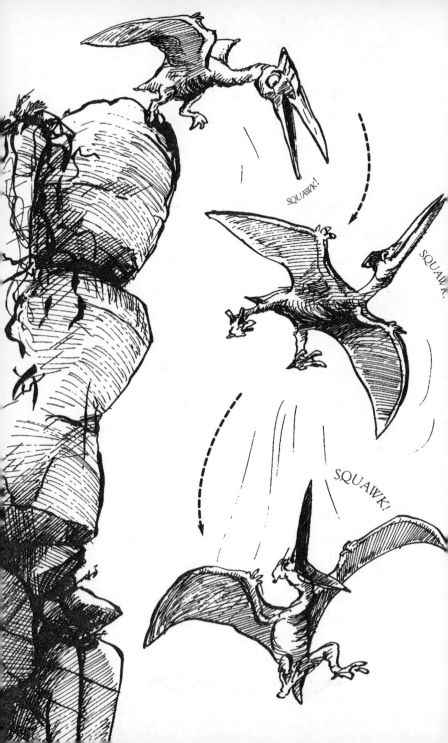

'Of course,' said Jamie. 'It's Quetzy Flying School. The mum's teaching them how to fly.'

'And the cliffs are a perfect launching site,' said Tom. 'Plenty of height.'

The third baby waddled to the edge, opened its wings wide and vanished from sight. The boys heard a squeal of triumph and the little quetzy reappeared, flapping its wings and squawking at its mother. The mum squawked back encouragingly. Then the baby flew in a large circle and headed off out to sea.

'Perhaps the mother will go off after them and we can rescue Wanna,' said Tom hopefully.

But now the mother quetzy was nudging Wanna towards the edge.

Jamie looked from Wanna to the cliff top. 'She wants him to fly too!'

'Uh oh,' Tom said. 'We've got to save him!'

67

They darted out from their hiding place. Wanna was squatting on the edge of the cliff. He grunked and flapped his front legs as if he had been watching the others.

AARK! The mother quetzy was getting impatient. She prodded Wanna and he nearly fell off the cliff.

Suddenly Jamie knew what to do.

'Grab him!' he yelled to Tom. 'We'll all jump down and aim for the ledge below. It's our only chance.'

Dodging under the mother quetzy's wings, the boys charged at Wanna, seized him round the middle and leapt off the cliff.

CHAPTER 6

Crunch!

They landed in a heap in the bouncy creepers. One of the babies was there and it squealed with delight when it saw Wanna appear in front of him. The boys gave each other a high five.

'We made it!'

AAARK!

'It's the mum,' said Jamie urgently, looking up.

The quetzy was peering over the edge of the cliff. She poked her long beak down and the boys had to roll out of the way. She opened her wings and took to the air. 'We'd better get out of here before she circles round to rescue her chick— and Wanna. But how are we going to get him to the beach?'

'Perhaps we can make a rope out of the creepers,' suggested Tom.

'Then we can lower him.'

'It would work as long as we tie good knots,' said Jamie.

Grunk, grunk!

They turned to see Wanna clambering to the far end of the ledge and disappearing from view.

'Wait, Wanna,' cried Tom, scrambling across to see where he'd gone. 'You'll fall!'

But to his surprise Wanna was trotting happily across the cliff face. He'd found a little trail that wound right down to the sand. The boys followed, placing each foot carefully on the narrow path.

'This is easier than the climb up,' said Tom.

'But not as exciting,' replied Jamie.

Swoosh! The mother quetzy swooped up past them, claws outstretched.

'She's come for her baby,' said Tom. 'I hope.'

The quetzy glided gracefully to the ledge

and soon had her chick in her grasp. She
made a wide, slow circle over the beach.
The boys held their breath.

Was she coming for Wanna now?

But after an anxious moment she rose to
the cliff top and disappeared.

As soon as the boys stepped onto the sand, Wanna bounded up and head butted them affectionately.

'Let's get you home, boy,' said Tom. 'Before your new mother comes looking for you.'

They set off back into the jungle, Wanna running alongside them, grunking happily.

As they followed the river back to Wanna's cave, Jamie stopped and wrinkled his nose. 'What's that smell?'

'It's Wanna,' Tom laughed. 'He's still covered in quetzy puke.'

'Yuck!' Jamie held his nose. 'Someone needs a bath.'

He waded into the shallows and held out a gingko. Wanna bounded into the river.

'Great,' said Tom, jumping in to join them. 'We can give him a shower.'

He cupped his hands in the water and splashed Wanna all over.

Then Wanna turned and thumped the surface with his tail. Jamie and Tom got soaked.

'Thanks, Wanna,' said Tom. 'At least that gross yellow puke has gone.'

Finally, they climbed out of the shadows and made their way up the hill to Wanna's cave.

Grunk.

Wanna ran straight to his nest and curled up.

'You've got the right nest this time,' grinned Jamie. He took the last gingkoes out of his bag and put them by Wanna's side. 'See you soon, little friend.'

They put their feet in the dinosaur footprints and walked backwards towards the cave wall into the smugglers' cave. They hurried out of the cave and down the headland, running all the way along the beach to the path that led up Sealight Head. After waiting a little while for the sun to dry out their clothes, they raced up the steps, two at a time, and burst through the door of the lighthouse.

'We must have been away ages,' gasped Jamie. 'Dad's done so much.'

They gazed at the breathtaking displays of dinosaur models and fossils all around the room.

77

'Awesome!' Tom pointed at a huge ammonite. 'It's as big as a tyre.'

Jamie wandered round, taking it all in. 'The triceratops skull looks great up on the wall.'

His dad came in at that moment, laden with books.

'Hello there, boys,' he called. 'Found anything out about the quetzy nest?'

The boys went over to the model Cretaceous landscape. 'We think it would have nested here on the cliff top,' said Jamie. 'There's lots of room for those huge wings and it's a perfect take-off point.'

'The babies could learn to fly from there,' added Tom eagerly. 'It's very high and there'd be uplift from the wind coming off the ocean.'

'Good thinking, boys,' said Jamie's dad. He placed the quetzalcoatlus carefully down on the cliff top. 'They'd be able to skim down over the sea and catch their dinner.'

Jamie looked at the quetzalcoatlus model, its wings outstretched ready for flight. He winked at Tom.

'That's not all they catch,' he whispered.

Far Away Mountains

Great Plains

Fang Rock

Crashing Rock Falls

Gingko Hill

GLOSSARY

Baculite (back-you-lite) – an extinct sea creature that swam upside down with its head sticking out from the bottom of its long thin shell. Because baculite fossils are fragile, fossil hunters rarely find a fossilized baculite shell intact.

Elasmosaurus (ee-laz-mow-sor-us) – a long-necked prehistoric sea creature with a small head, sharp teeth and four flippers. Elasmosaurus may have stretched 14 metres long, with its neck making up half of its total length.

Gingko (gink-oh) – a tree native to China called a 'living fossil' because fossils of it have been found dating back millions of years, yet they are still around today. Also known as the stink bomb tree because of its smelly apricot-like fruit.

Platecarpus (plat-ee-carp-us) – an extinct sharp-toothed lizard with a long, flat tail and flippers which may have swum like a snake in prehistoric waters.

Pterosaur (ter-oh-sor) – a prehistoric flying reptile. Its wings were leathery and light and some of these 'winged lizards' had fur on their bodies and bony crests on their heads.

Quetzalcoatlus (ket-sal-kow-at-lus) – one of the largest flying animals ever. Named after the Aztec feathered serpent god Quetzalcoatl, this prehistoric bird had a long neck, toothless jaw and a long bony crest on top of its head. Its clawed wings could span up to 15 metres across.

Wannanosaurus (wah-nan-oh-sor-us) – a dinosaur that only ate plants and used its hard, flat skull to defend itself. Named after the place it was discovered: Wannano in China.

DINOSAUR COVE™

CATCHING THE SPEEDY THIEF

by
REX STONE

illustrated by
MIKE SPOOR

Series created by
Working Partners Ltd

OXFORD
UNIVERSITY PRESS

Special thanks to Jane Clarke

For Guy Macdonald, a true explorer of adventures

FACT FILE

➡️ JAMIE HAS JUST MOVED FROM THE CITY TO LIVE IN THE LIGHTHOUSE IN DINOSAUR COVE. JAMIE'S DAD IS OPENING A DINOSAUR MUSEUM ON THE BOTTOM FLOOR OF THE LIGHTHOUSE. WHEN JAMIE GOES HUNTING FOR FOSSILS IN THE CRUMBLING CLIFFS ON THE BEACH HE MEETS A LOCAL BOY, TOM, AND THE TWO DISCOVER AN AMAZING SECRET: A WORLD WITH REAL, LIVE DINOSAURS! THE BOYS HAVE EXPLORED THE JUNGLE, THE MARSH, AND THE CLIFFS, BUT WHEN THEY SPEND TIME AT THE LAGOON, THEY END UP FISHING FOR TROUBLE!

JAMIE

- **FULL NAME:** JAMIE MORGAN
- **AGE:** 8 YEARS
- **SIZE:** 1 JATOM*
- **TOP SPEED:** 10 KPH
- **LIKES:** FOSSIL HUNTING AND LEARNING ABOUT DINOSAURS
- **DISLIKES:** BEING STUCK INDOORS

Jamie's eye

Jamie's foot

Jamie's hand

*NOTE: A JATOM IS THE SIZE OF JAMIE OR TOM: 125 CM TALL AND 27 KG IN WEIGHT

TOM

- **FULL NAME:** THOMAS CLAY
- **AGE:** 8 YEARS
- **SIZE:** 1 JATOM*
- **TOP SPEED:** 10 KPH
- **LIKES:** TRACKING ANIMALS AND EXPLORING WILDLIFE
- **DISLIKES:** RAINY DAYS

Tom's eye   Tom's hand

WANNA

- **FULL NAME:** WANNANOSAURUS
- **AGE:** 65 – 80 MILLION YEARS**
- **SIZE:** LESS THAN A JATOM*
- **TOP SPEED:** 50 KPH, ESPECIALLY WHEN BEING CHASED BY A T-REX
- **LIKES:** STINKY GINGKO FRUIT AND BANGING HIS HEAD ON TREE TRUNKS
- **DISLIKES:** SCARY DINOSAURS

Wanna's head   Wanna's foot

*NOTE: A JATOM IS THE SIZE OF JAMIE OR TOM: 125 CM TALL AND 27 KG IN WEIGHT
**NOTE: SCIENTISTS CALL THIS PERIOD THE LATE CRETACEOUS

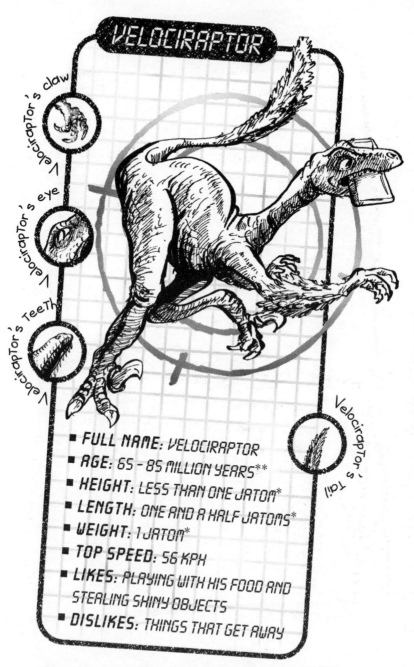

VELOCIRAPTOR

Velociraptor's claw

Velociraptor's eye

Velociraptor's Teeth

Velociraptor's Tail

- **FULL NAME:** VELOCIRAPTOR
- **AGE:** 65 - 85 MILLION YEARS**
- **HEIGHT:** LESS THAN ONE JATOM*
- **LENGTH:** ONE AND A HALF JATOMS*
- **WEIGHT:** 1 JATOM*
- **TOP SPEED:** 56 KPH
- **LIKES:** PLAYING WITH HIS FOOD AND STEALING SHINY OBJECTS
- **DISLIKES:** THINGS THAT GET AWAY

*NOTE: A JATOM IS THE SIZE OF JAMIE OR TOM: 125 CM TALL AND 27 KG IN WEIGHT
**NOTE: SCIENTISTS CALL THIS PERIOD THE LATE CRETACEOUS

DINOSAUR COVE

Village

Marina

Sealight Head

Landslips where clay and fossils are

Muddy beach

DINO CAVE

High Tide beach line

Low Tide beach line

Sea

Smuggler's Point

89

CHAPTER 1

Jamie Morgan pulled a rainbow-coloured metal fish out of his grandad's tackle box and held it up for his friend Tom Clay to see. 'This fish has feathers!' A cluster of tiny pink and orange feathers sprouted out from where the tail should be.

'Different baits catch different beasts,' Jamie's grandad said with a grin, holding out his hand for the feathery fish. 'This spinner is great for catching sea bass. Now, let's see. What else will I need today?'

sea bass spinner

crab line

He tipped a tangle of weights, spinners, and fishing line onto the kitchen floor of the old lighthouse.

'What's this?' Jamie picked up an H-shaped piece of orange plastic with string wrapped around it and a couple of heavy lead weights dangling from it.

'Haven't you seen one before?' Tom said in amazement. 'It's a crab line.'

Jamie shook his head. 'How can this catch crabs?'

'It's easy,' Tom said. 'You tie a bit of bacon rind on the end and throw it in. The crabs grab the bacon and you grab the crabs!'

'Cool!' said Jamie. 'I'd like to try that.'

'The best place for crabbing is Sealight Head at high tide,' Grandad said, as he crammed everything but the crab line back in his tackle box. 'But high tide isn't until later this afternoon. I'll meet you there, if you like, after I've caught some sea bass for dinner.'

'OK, Grandad,' Jamie said as the old man finished packing his tackle box. 'We'll wait until then.'

'We don't have to wait,' Tom whispered to Jamie. 'We could go crabbing in Misty Lagoon in Dino World right now.'

Dino World was Jamie and Tom's secret—even Grandad didn't know that they'd found a world where real live dinosaurs lived.

'Great idea!' Jamie winked at Tom. 'We'll meet you near Sealight Head later, Grandad.'

'Don't forget the bait and mop bucket to put the crabs in,' Grandad told them. He pulled on his fishing boots. 'And I've put two cheese and pickle sandwiches in the fridge for you.' He headed for the door. 'Have fun!'

'We will,' Tom said with a smile. The minute Grandad was out of the door Tom grabbed the handle of the mop bucket. 'Got your Fossil Finder, Jamie?'

'Already in my backpack.' Jamie grinned as he wrapped two cheese and pickle sandwiches in shiny tinfoil and made a separate package for the bacon. He stuffed them in his backpack along with the crab line. 'Let's go!'

The boys clattered down the
stairs of the lighthouse and dashed
through the dinosaur exhibits on
the ground floor. Jamie's dad was
busy fixing a label to the wall next
to the triceratops skull.

'How's the museum going,
Mr Morgan?' Tom asked.

'Great, thanks,' said Jamie's
dad. 'The Grand Opening is only
a few days away.'

'See ya, Dad!' Jamie called, hurrying past the Late Cretaceous model and the T-Rex display. 'We're going crabbing.'

The boys scrambled down the rocky path from the lighthouse and ran along the beach onto the trail that led up Smuggler's Point. They bent double to catch their breath, and then clambered up the boulders to the smugglers' cave and squeezed through the gap at the back into the secret chamber.

'This is my favourite place in the whole world!' Jamie's heart began to pound as soon as he placed his feet into the fossilized dinosaur footprints on the cave floor.

'One . . . two . . . three . . . ' He counted each step. 'Keep close behind me, Tom.'

'You bet.' Tom's voice sounded excited. 'I wonder what we're going to find this time.'

'Four . . .'

A crack of light appeared in the cave wall in front of him. 'Five!' The ground squelched beneath Jamie's feet and he stood blinking in the bright sunshine and breathing in the familiar warm wet-leaf smell of Dino World.

A second later, Jamie and Tom were standing on Gingko Hill, and a rough, slobbery tongue was licking Jamie's hand.

'Ready for another adventure, Wanna?' Jamie asked their little dinosaur friend.

Jamie picked a stinky gingko fruit and held it out to the wannanosaurus.

Wanna took it gently, then greedily gobbled it up, wagging his tail and grunking as smelly gingko juice dribbled down his chin.

'It's almost like he was waiting for us,' Tom said with a laugh.

With Tom and Wanna close behind, Jamie strode through the trees to a curtain of creepers at the edge of Gingko Hill. As he pushed the creepers aside, excitement fizzed like soda in his stomach.

Beneath them lay the steamy emerald-green jungle. The air throbbed with the whirring and buzzing of insects, and the jungle rang with the strange calls of the weird and wonderful creatures that only lived in Dino World.

'This has got to be the best place for adventures in the whole wide world!' Jamie announced with a huge grin on his face.

'In the whole solar system!' Tom cheered.

'In the whole universe!' Jamie exclaimed.

Wanna grunked his agreement.

'Come on!' Jamie said. 'Let's see what we can catch in Misty Lagoon. We've only got until the tide comes in.'

The three friends clambered down the steep hillside into the dense jungle.

'We can follow the stream,' Jamie said, jumping into the shallow water that trickled and gurgled its way to the lagoon.

They splashed along the stream bed.

'That's where we met the T-Rex,' Tom said, pointing to a jumble of huge rounded rocks.

'I'll never forget those fangs.' Jamie shuddered. 'I hope he's not around today.'

'Me too,' said Tom, looking round nervously. 'Let's get a move on.'

They ran until they burst out of the jungle onto the palm-fringed sandy beach of the sparkling blue lagoon.

Jamie shaded his eyes with his hand and gazed round the shore. 'Which would be the best spot to find prehistoric crabs?'

'We need deep water for crabbing,' Tom told him. 'It's no use wading into the shallows.'

'How about over there?' Jamie pointed to an outcrop of fern-covered rocks on the north-east shore. A stone ledge stuck out of the ferns like a wide diving board, hanging over the deep, blue water.

'Perfect!' Tom declared.

Jamie led the way around the lagoon to the rocks and scrambled on top of them, pushing aside the

plants. It was an easy climb to the ledge over the water, and he put down his backpack in the shade of the tall ferns.

Tom scrambled up onto the ledge next to him. 'We can't see much through these ferns,' he said, glancing over his shoulder. 'But Wanna will warn us if anything tries to sneak up.'

He leaned over the lagoon and filled up the bucket with water. 'Time to bait the line.'

Jamie knelt on the rock ledge and dug inside his backpack.

'Here's the bacon.' Jamie handed Tom a tinfoil packet and then unravelled the crab line.

Wanna watched curiously as Tom unwrapped the bacon.

'No, Wanna, it's not for you,' Tom told the little dinosaur, tearing off the bacon rind. Wanna leaned over Tom's shoulder. His long tongue shot towards the bacon.

Gak gak gak!

Wanna spluttered in disgust. He spun around and grabbed a mouthful of fern leaves.

'He's trying to get rid of the taste,' Jamie said, tying the bacon rind onto the end of the line. 'Plant eaters don't eat bacon.'

Tom showed Jamie how to hold the
orange plastic handle and carefully lower
the crab line into the lagoon. Jamie felt
the string run through his fingers until the
weight came to rest on the bottom.

'Do I pull it up straight away?' he
asked.

'No.' Tom laughed. 'You have to be
patient. You'll feel a tug on the line when
something takes the bait.'

'What if it isn't a crab?' Jamie asked.
'What if it's a huge electric eel?'

'Ooh,' Tom said. 'What if it's a humongous stingray?'

'What if it's a Loch Ness monster with ginormous fangs?' As Jamie laughed, a big bubble broke the mirror surface of the water.

Pop!

Jamie leapt to his feet, startling Wanna, who nearly fell backwards over the bucket.

But there was no giant creature leaping out at them. The lagoon was a calm mirror once more.

'False alarm,' Tom said. 'There's nothing there.'

Wanna started to chew a fern stem.

'Wanna's got the right idea,' Jamie said. 'Let's have lunch while we wait.'

'Good idea.' Tom rummaged in the backpack and pulled out the tinfoil packet. He took out a sandwich and handed it to Jamie.

'Your grandad's pickle is great!' Tom mumbled with his mouth full. 'Even if it does blow your head off,' he said between coughs.

'It is a bit spicy,' Jamie agreed, taking a huge bite. He felt a tug on the crab line. 'Something's taken the bait!' he spluttered, spraying a mouthful of crumbs all over the rock. He threw down his sandwich and

started to pull up the line
as fast as he could. The line
went limp.

Tom and Jamie peered
over the ledge. 'It got
away,' Jamie realized, as
the end of the empty line
came out of the water.
'It ate the bacon, too.'

'Better luck next
time.' Tom tore off
another strip of
bacon and fixed it to the
dripping line. Jamie threw it back
in the water and reached for his sandwich.

'Where's my sandwich gone?' he said.
There was a rustle in the ferns. Jamie whirled
round in time to see the ferns stirring as a
creature scurried away through them.

'Wanna!' Jamie yelled. 'You sandwich thief!'

Jamie gave the handle of the crab line to
Tom and hopped off the rock into the ferns. He
could hear a strange high-pitched rattling noise.

Ack ack ack!

'Wanna?' he called. 'Is that you?'

The ferns parted. The little dinosaur
was bobbing his head and hopping excitedly

from foot to foot. His tongue was hanging out and he was making strange noises.

Jamie knew what that meant: Wanna must have been spluttering on Grandad's pickle. 'It's your own fault. You shouldn't have stolen my sandwich,' Jamie scolded him.

'Come quick!' Tom shouted from behind him. 'We've caught something

big!'

CHAPTER 3

'One, two, three… heave!'

Jamie and Tom pulled on the crab line with all their might.

'Look at the size of that!' Tom gasped.

Dangling from the crab line was the biggest crab that Jamie had ever seen. Its shell was the size of a dinner plate. The crab's silvery shell shone in the sunshine as it held tight to the bacon on the end of the line. As Tom held the line, Jamie grabbed the bucket.

Wanna edged up and sniffed at the crab.
It waved a pincer at him.

Grunk!

Wanna jumped back in alarm as Tom
lowered the crab gently into the bucket.

'It's a good job this is a big bucket.'
Jamie laughed.

They peered into the bucket.
The crab was using its pincers
to tear off small pieces of the
bacon and shovel them
into its mouth.

'Crabs haven't changed much since dino times,' Tom said thoughtfully.

Jamie took out his Fossil Finder and flipped it open. The '*HAPPY HUNTING*' screen popped up and he tapped *CRAB* into the search

CRAB

SEARCH: CRAB

box. ' *"CRABS HAVEN'T CHANGED MUCH SINCE DINOSAUR TIMES,"* '
he read aloud.

Tom laughed. 'That's what I said.'

Jamie snapped shut the Fossil Finder and put it on the rock beside him. 'I want to take a close look at this dino crab,' he told Tom. 'Help me get it off the line. It's wedged in the bucket, so it shouldn't nip us.'

Tom held the bucket steady and Jamie untangled the line from the crab's pincers.

Just when he had finished, there was a sudden rustle in the ferns behind them.

Ack ack ack!

Jamie spun round to see what was making the noise. A turkey-sized dinosaur with open toothy jaws dashed out from the plants onto the ledge beside them.

Tom almost dropped the bucket in surprise.

Snap!

The new dinosaur grabbed the Fossil Finder
in its needle-sharp fangs.

Ack ack ack ack ack!

With a whip of the feathers on
the end of its long yellow and
orange tail, the two-legged
dinosaur turned and darted
into the ferns.

Snap!

'What was that?' Tom said, still holding the bucket.

'Th-that . . . ' stammered Jamie, feeling the blood drain from his face, 'that was a velociraptor. A velociraptor just stole my Fossil Finder!'

Tom looked startled.

'We have to get it back,' Jamie said, shoving the crab line into his backpack.

Jamie crashed into the tall ferns and raced after the rapidly retreating raptor. Tom and Wanna plunged after him.

'It's heading towards the Far Away Mountains,' Tom said, as they emerged from the ferns into a section of the plains they hadn't been to before.

'Why did you bring the crab?' Jamie asked as they puffed along a shallow stream that flowed down to the lagoon.

Tom looked down in amazement at the

bucket that swung from his hand. 'Forgot I
had it,' he said. 'I'll take it back later.'

Ahead of them, the velociraptor darted
into a narrow passageway where the stream
gushed between two huge rocks.

'Careful,' Tom said. 'We don't know what's
on the other side of the rocks.'

'Time to find out.' Jamie stepped into the
cool, fast-moving stream. Edging sideways like
a crab, he squeezed through the narrow gap,
followed closely by Tom and Wanna.

'Wow,' he breathed. 'It's like a rainbow!'

Ahead, the stream flowed through a rocky
area streaked with splashes of bright orange,
yellow, and green mud and cratered with deep
blue pools that sparkled in the sunshine.

'There's the raptor!' Tom pointed to a reptilian tail disappearing into a cave on the other side of the pools.

'That must be where it lives.' Jamie heaved a sigh of relief. 'Urgh!' he sputtered. 'It stinks of rotten eggs around here.'

'Wanna likes it,' Tom said, glancing at the little dinosaur. Wanna was standing next to one of the small pools with his snout in the air, sniffing deeply.

'He would,' Jamie laughed. 'He likes anything stinky.'

Wanna cocked his head to one side and peered into the pool.

'Is he looking for more crabs?'

As Tom spoke, Wanna's pool burbled and bubbled. Pop! A wisp of hot steam escaped from a burst bubble and the smell of rotten eggs welled up.

'The water's hot,' Jamie chuckled.
'The only crabs he'll find in there
will be bright pink cooked ones.'

Suddenly, there was a great

whoosh!

Wanna leapt back from the pool
as a column of steaming water gushed
high into the air.

Jamie watched it, mesmerized.

'Get out of the way!' Tom yelled
as the column collapsed and a
torrent of scalding water
fell towards them.

Jamie, Tom, and Wanna dived behind a rock as scalding drops of water rained down.

'It's a geyser,' Tom said excitedly. 'I saw one on a TV programme about Yellowstone Park. The water's heated up by melted rock that bubbles up from the centre of the earth.'

The boys and Wanna peered out from behind the rock. On the other side of the pools, near the raptor's cave, there was a hissing and popping like a champagne cork and another geyser whooshed and spurted

into the air. Each of the six pools took their turn to shoot jets of hot water and steam into the air.

'No wonder that velociraptor's chosen to live in this cave,' murmured Tom. 'What other dinosaur would be fast enough to run past all the boiling geysers?'

'If we're careful, we can do it,' Jamie said. 'We've got to get the Fossil Finder back. If we leave it behind here, it might get fossilized— then someone in the future could dig up a computer next to a dinosaur fossil. We'll just have to learn the geysers' pattern.'

osh!

The boys watched as the geysers repeated their eruptions.

'I think I got it,' Jamie said.

The valley had gone quiet again. The only sound was the stream. It was as if nothing had happened.

'Now!' Tom yelled, clutching the crab bucket to his chest.

The boys and Wanna sprinted past the first pool.

Whoosh!

The huge geyser shot into the air behind them.

Whoosh!

'Watch out!' Jamie shouted. The three jumped into the stream and hid under an overhanging rock as the hot rain pattered into the water. As soon as it had passed, Wanna darted out and dashed past the second pool and the third, dodging the bubbling water.

'Follow Wanna!' Jamie yelled to Tom, and they raced after their dinosaur friend as all around them steaming fountains of scalding water exploded from mini-geysers.

Whoosh!

In front of the cave, an
aquamarine pool began to gurgle.

Whoosh!

'Geyser about to blow!' Tom shouted
above the sound of the fast-flowing
stream. Jamie, Tom, and Wanna
sprinted past the gurgling
pool and hurled
themselves behind a
rock at the edge of the
cave mouth as the
last geyser exploded
with a whoosh!

'That was close.'

Tom caught his breath and then peered into the bucket. 'The dino crab seems to be OK. It's waving its pincers, though. I think it's annoyed.'

'I'm not surprised.' Jamie grinned, glancing at his watch. 'We have to hurry,' he told Tom. 'It'll be high tide soon. We've got to get back before Grandad comes looking for us.'

'Sshh!' Tom whispered. 'Wanna can hear something.'

Wanna was peering into the cave with his tail sticking out stiffly behind him.

Ack ack ack ack ack!

A high-pitched rattle came from the back of the cave. Wanna shot backwards, making grunking noises.

'Hide!' Jamie hissed. The boys and Wanna ducked back behind the rock but nothing came out of the cave.

'We'll have to be careful,' Tom whispered, gently putting down the crab bucket. 'That's the raptor's den, and animals are dangerous if you corner them in their den.'

They peered into the cave. Against the wall, near the entrance, was a nest like a bird's, but woven from dried ferns, and the size of a car tyre. The sun was sparkling on shiny objects set among the brown stalks and leaves.

'Velociraptors must collect shiny things, like magpies,' Tom said. 'I can see the Fossil Finder!'

Jamie breathed a sigh of relief. 'It's really close and there's no sign of the raptor. He must have gone deeper into the cave. Maybe we can just grab the Fossil Finder and get out of here.'

Tom nodded. 'Let's try.'
They quietly crept into
the gloomy, dank cave and
tiptoed towards the velociraptor's nest.
Jamie's foot crunched on something. *Ugh!*
He looked down and shuddered. Well-gnawed
bones were scattered around the huge nest.

'It's like the nest of a giant bird of prey,'
Tom whispered from behind him. 'If that
raptor gets us, we're in big trouble.'

A prickle of fear ran down Jamie's spine.
He knew they had to be very careful.

Suddenly, the velociraptor shot out of the
darkness, snarling viciously.

Ack ack ack ack ack!

CHAPTER 5

Jamie threw himself backwards as the raptor pounced.

Snap!

The raptor's needle-sharp teeth closed on empty air.

'Get out, quick!' Tom grabbed Jamie by the T-shirt and pulled him out of the cave and back behind the rock, nearly knocking over the dino crab bucket in the process.

Once more, they peered around the rock with Wanna grunking softly behind them.

Ack ack ack ack ack!

The velociraptor was rattling softly to itself as it bent over its nest and carefully rearranged the position of the Fossil Finder in pride of place in the centre. The whoosh of the geysers exploded down the valley, drowning out all sound.

'If we lure it out of the cave,' Jamie whispered to Tom, 'then I can dash in and grab the Fossil Finder.'

'We lured the ankylosaurus out of the mud with flowers,' Tom said. 'But the velociraptor is a carnivore.'

Jamie glanced at the crab in the bucket. 'I've got an idea!' He rummaged in his backpack, took out the crab line and tied on the remains of the bacon.

'Cool!' Tom grinned, taking the line. 'I've never crabbed for dinosaurs before.'

Tom scrambled up onto the rocks above the cave and lowered the crab line so that the bacon dangled at raptor height in the mouth of the cave.

The valley quietened again as Jamie and Wanna flattened themselves behind the rock at the side of the cave entrance. Wanna grunked softly to himself.

'We have to be patient for crabbing,' Jamie told the little dinosaur.

Suddenly, the raptor lunged out of the mouth of the cave reaching for the bacon

with its sharp talons, but Tom jerked the crab line up and away.

The raptor spread the feathers on its tail and forelimbs and launched itself into the air after the meat, but it was too high. Tom lowered the bacon again to just in front of the vicious dinosaur, but pulled it away before it could grab it. The raptor leapt again and boxed at the bacon on the end of the line.

'It's like a kitten playing with a piece of string,' Jamie whispered to Wanna.

Tom edged along the rock shelf above the mouth of the cave, taking the bacon bait further and further away from where Jamie and Wanna were hiding.

'It worked!' Jamie said.

He darted into the cave and grabbed the Fossil Finder out of the nest. He was about to hurry away when he spotted the foil that had been wrapped around his sandwich—it had been the raptor that stole his sandwich, not Wanna!

I can't leave that to get fossilized, he thought, snatching it up. Jamie kept to the shadows and crept back the way he had come.

So far, so good, he thought, and he poked his head cautiously out of the cave.

140

Instead of seeing Wanna's friendly face, two cold reptilian eyes stared unblinkingly back at him.

'Oh no!' Jamie breathed.

The velociraptor was back. It tilted its head to one side.

Ack ack ack!

The raptor rattled ominously and began to twitch its tail from side to side.

Ack
ack
ack!

Jamie's blood ran cold. It looked like a cat preparing to pounce on its prey.

'It's going to attack!' Tom screamed from the ledge above as the velociraptor spread its talon-like claws and came towards Jamie.

Jamie froze to the spot. Any moment now, the raptor's sharp teeth and claws would tear him to pieces.

Something scratched at the ground behind him. Jamie whirled round. Wanna! Wanna was revving up, getting a claw hold on the rock, his bony head lowered . . .

Gaaaaak!

The little dinosaur charged just as the velociraptor sprang at Jamie.

Thwack!

Wanna barged into the velociraptor and bowled it over.

As the raptor spat and rattled furiously, struggling to get back to its feet, Jamie and Wanna raced behind the rock.

'Mind the crab!' Jamie yelled. Too late. Wanna's tail smacked into the bucket and knocked it over. Jamie watched as the large dino crab tumbled out, pinched its claws at him, and scuttled away. It headed towards the stream, its silvery shell sparkling in the sunshine.

The stunned raptor stood up, shook itself, and looked around menacingly. Its tail feathers stiffened as it spotted the silvery crab scuttling past.

The raptor lunged after the crab. The crab darted this way and that as the raptor chased it.

146

'See! Raptors like shiny things!' Tom yelled from the ledge above the cave as the raptor turned, crouched and sprang towards the crab.

Snap!

The raptor's teeth crunched together on thin air.

Dino Crab hasn't got a chance, Jamie thought, but then stared in amazement as the crab waved its pincers defiantly at the raptor, rushed towards it, and pinched it on the calf of its left leg.

Ack! The raptor leapt back in surprise and pain.

'Go, Dino Crab!' the boys cheered, as the crab scuttled away from the raptor, towards the tumbling cool stream. They watched it plop into the water and sail like a boat downstream towards Misty Lagoon.

The
velociraptor
raced after the crab,
dodging spouts of hot
steam as one after another
the geysers erupted all
around it.

'Dino Crab can take care
of itself.' Tom laughed. 'That
velociraptor has met its match!'
Jamie looked at his watch.
'We better get back,' he yelled
up to Tom.

'I can see Gingko Hill from up here,'
Tom called down. 'We can go across
the plains.'

'Great!' Jamie grabbed the bucket
and he and Wanna clambered up onto the
rock ledge above the cave. As they climbed,
the green top of Gingko Hill rose in the
distance. 'I'm glad we don't have to go back
through the geysers.'

Wanna greeted Tom with a wag of his tail,
then strode off along the narrow path that led
away from the cave. At the top, Jamie put
down the bucket and shaded his eyes to look

out across the gently rolling plains that lay
between them and Gingko Hill. On the edge
of the plains, a herd of small stocky dinosaurs
with big bony neck frills and parrot-like beaks
was grazing peacefully on the horsetail ferns.

Jamie rummaged in his backpack and took
out the Fossil Finder. Its shiny case was
dented with raptor tooth marks. He rubbed
off a streak of dried raptor dribble and then
flipped it open.

'It still works,' he said in relief as he typed in '*NECK FRILL*' and '*BEAK*'.

Tom looked over his shoulder. '*PROTOCERATOPS*,' he read. 'They're harmless.' He put the crab line in the bucket and picked it up. 'And they wouldn't be browsing if any carnivores were around.'

Wanna bobbed his head as if in agreement, turned, and set off towards Gingko Hill followed by Tom. Jamie snapped the Fossil Finder shut, crammed it into his backpack, and hurried after them.

'He knows all the paths around here,' Tom said as Wanna confidently led them past the herd of peaceful protoceratops and through the jumbles of rock and tangles of tree ferns that littered the plains. They followed the little dinosaur across the stream and back up the conifer-carpeted hillside to the top of Gingko Hill.

Jamie checked his watch.
'We should make it in time to
meet Grandad,' he said, giving
Wanna a pat on the head.
'Bye, Wanna, see you next
time. Sorry I accused you of
stealing my sandwich.'

Jamie picked a handful of
gingko fruit and the little
dinosaur grunked happily as
he settled down by his nest
and began to munch on the
stinky fruit.

Tom looked at his watch.
'We'll have to hurry,'
he announced.

The boys carefully placed their feet in the fresh dinosaur prints outside the rock face and stepped backwards out of the bright sunshine of Dino World into the darkness of the smugglers' cave. They squeezed through the gap, dashed out of the cave, and burst out onto Smuggler's Point. Beneath them the waves were swirling close to the rocks.

'The beach will be cut off any minute,' Tom said. 'It's almost high tide.'

They sprinted down the path and reached the beach just as the first gentle waves lapped at the bottom of the pathway.

'Just in time!' Jamie shouted, as they splashed through the shallow water and hurried to the other side of the cove.

'Ahoy there, me hearties!' Grandad greeted them with a wave from the rocks beneath Sealight Head. 'Are you ready for a crabbing adventure?'

'Just as long as there are no geysers or raptors,' Tom whispered to Jamie as they scrambled up the rocks to join him.

Jamie grinned. 'Ahoy there, Grandad,' he called. 'We're always ready for a new adventure!'

Ahoy There, me hearTies!

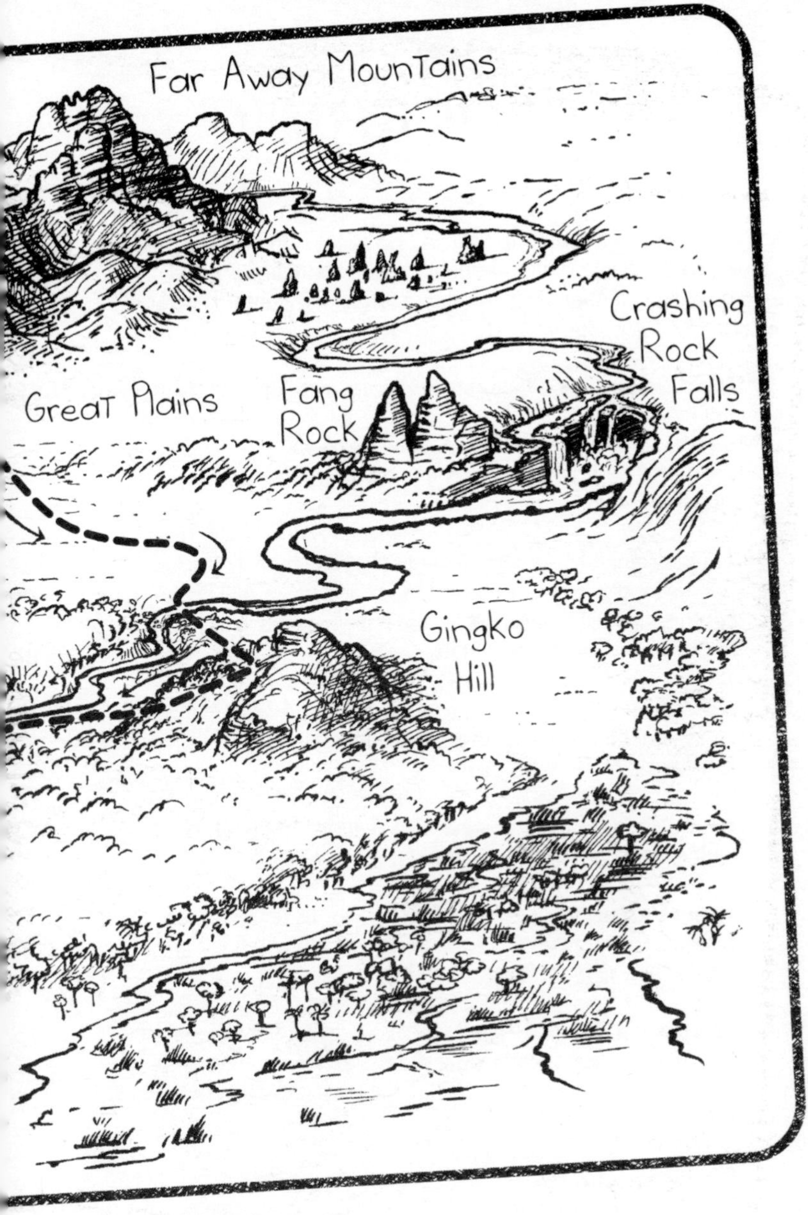

Far Away Mountains

Great Plains

Fang Rock

Crashing Rock Falls

Gingko Hill

GLOSSARY

Ankylosaurus (an-ki-low-sor-us) – a vegetarian dinosaur known for its armoured coat and clubbed tail. Its armour consisted of large bony bumps similar to the covering of modern-day crocodiles and lizards.

Fossil Finder – hand-held computer filled with dinosaur facts.

Geyser (gee-ser) – a hot spring, heated by volcanic activity below the earth's surface, that erupts in a tall stream of hot water and steam from time to time.

Gingko (gink-oh) – a tree native to China called a 'living fossil' because fossils of it have been found dating back millions of years, yet they are still around today. Also known as the stink bomb tree because of its smelly apricot-like fruit.

Protoceratops (pro-toe-serra-tops) – a horned, plant-eating dinosaur with a large head, neck frill and parrot-like beak, roughly half the size of a triceratops.

Triceratops (T-tops) (try-serra-tops) – a three-horned, plant-eating dinosaur which looks like a rhinoceros.

Tyrannosaurus Rex (T-Rex) (ti-ran-oh-sor-us rex) – a meat-eating dinosaur with a huge tail, two strong legs but two tiny arms. T-Rex was one of the biggest, scariest dinosaurs.

Velociraptor (ve-loss-i-rap-tor) – meat-eating dinosaur which was one of the smartest and fastest dinosaurs. Velociraptors were about the size of a turkey with a large curved claw on both of its feet.

Wannanosaurus (wah-nan-oh-sor-us) – a dinosaur that only ate plants and used its hard, flat skull to defend itself. Named after the place it was discovered: Wannano in China.

DINOSAUR COVE™

STAMPEDE OF THE GIANT REPTILES

by
REX STONE

illustrated by
MIKE SPOOR

Series created by
Working Partners Ltd

OXFORD
UNIVERSITY PRESS

With special thanks to Jan Burchett and Sara Vogler

Thank you, also, to Mark Ford of the British and Irish Meteorite Society for his patient and helpful advice.

For Grandpa Dillon R.S.

These illustrations are for you Christopher.
Enjoy the adventure! M.S.

FACT FILE

➡ JAMIE HAS JUST MOVED FROM THE CITY TO LIVE IN THE LIGHTHOUSE IN DINOSAUR COVE. JAMIE'S DAD IS OPENING A DINOSAUR MUSEUM ON THE BOTTOM FLOOR OF THE LIGHTHOUSE. WHEN JAMIE GOES HUNTING FOR FOSSILS IN THE CRUMBLING CLIFFS ON THE BEACH HE MEETS A LOCAL BOY, TOM, AND THE TWO DISCOVER AN AMAZING SECRET: A WORLD WITH REAL, LIVE DINOSAURS! BUT THE BOYS HAVE TO WATCH OUT FOR FALLING OBJECTS AND STAMPEDES!

JAMIE

- **FULL NAME:** JAMIE MORGAN
- **AGE:** 8 YEARS
- **SIZE:** 1 JATOM*
- **TOP SPEED:** 10 KPH
- **LIKES:** FOSSIL HUNTING AND LEARNING ABOUT DINOSAURS
- **DISLIKES:** BEING STUCK INDOORS

Jamie's eye

Jamie's foot

Jamie's hand

*NOTE: A JATOM IS THE SIZE OF JAMIE OR TOM: 125 CM TALL AND 27 KG IN WEIGHT

TOM

- **FULL NAME:** THOMAS CLAY
- **AGE:** 8 YEARS
- **SIZE:** 1 JATOM*
- **TOP SPEED:** 10 KPH
- **LIKES:** TRACKING ANIMALS AND EXPLORING WILDLIFE
- **DISLIKES:** RAINY DAYS

Tom's eye

Tom's hand

WANNA

- **FULL NAME:** WANNANOSAURUS
- **AGE:** 65 – 80 MILLION YEARS**
- **SIZE:** LESS THAN A JATOM*
- **TOP SPEED:** 50 KPH, ESPECIALLY WHEN BEING CHASED BY A T-REX
- **LIKES:** STINKY GINGKO FRUIT AND BANGING HIS HEAD ON TREE TRUNKS
- **DISLIKES:** SCARY DINOSAURS

Wanna's head

Wanna's foot

*NOTE: A JATOM IS THE SIZE OF JAMIE OR TOM: 125 CM TALL AND 27 KG IN WEIGHT
**NOTE: SCIENTISTS CALL THIS PERIOD THE LATE CRETACEOUS

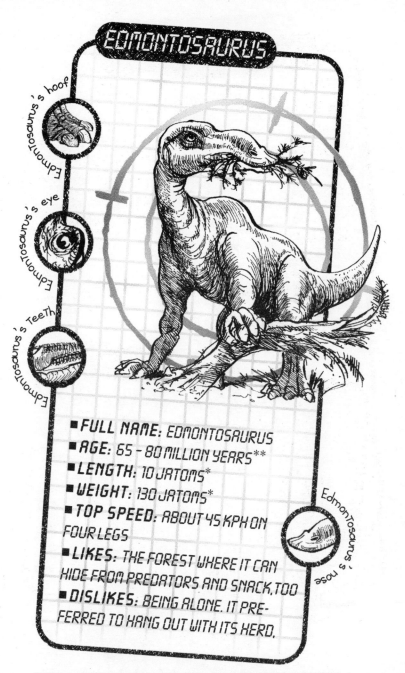

EDMONTOSAURUS

Edmontosaurus's hoof

Edmontosaurus's eye

Edmontosaurus's Teeth

Edmontosaurus's nose

- **FULL NAME:** EDMONTOSAURUS
- **AGE:** 65 – 80 MILLION YEARS**
- **LENGTH:** 10 JATOMS*
- **WEIGHT:** 130 JATOMS*
- **TOP SPEED:** ABOUT 45 KPH ON FOUR LEGS
- **LIKES:** THE FOREST WHERE IT CAN HIDE FROM PREDATORS AND SNACK, TOO
- **DISLIKES:** BEING ALONE. IT PREFERRED TO HANG OUT WITH ITS HERD.

*NOTE: A JATOM IS THE SIZE OF JAMIE OR TOM: 125 CM TALL AND 27 KG IN WEIGHT

**NOTE: SCIENTISTS CALL THIS PERIOD THE LATE CRETACEOUS

DINOSAUR COVE

Village

Marina

Sealight Head

Landslips where clay and fossils are

Muddy beach

DINO CAVE

High Tide beach line

Sea

Smuggler's Point

CHAPTER 1

Jamie Morgan stared at the huge dinosaur towering over him.

'That is awesome!' he exclaimed to his best friend Tom. 'A life-sized model of an edmontosaurus skeleton.'

The gigantic skeleton only just fitted in the museum on the ground floor of Jamie's lighthouse home. Its huge tail curled round the whitewashed walls and it reared up so that its duck-billed nose was high over the boys' heads. The museum was finally ready.

A big banner hung outside the lighthouse:
**Dinosaur Cove Museum Grand Opening
Today, One O'Clock**. This was the day
everyone had been waiting for.

FLASH!   FLASH!   FLASH!

Jamie and Tom blinked in surprise. The
photographer from the county paper was
aiming her camera at the edmontosaurus.
They jumped aside.

'It's OK, boys,' she called, waving an arm.
'Let's have you in the shot. It'll show readers
just how big this beast really was.'

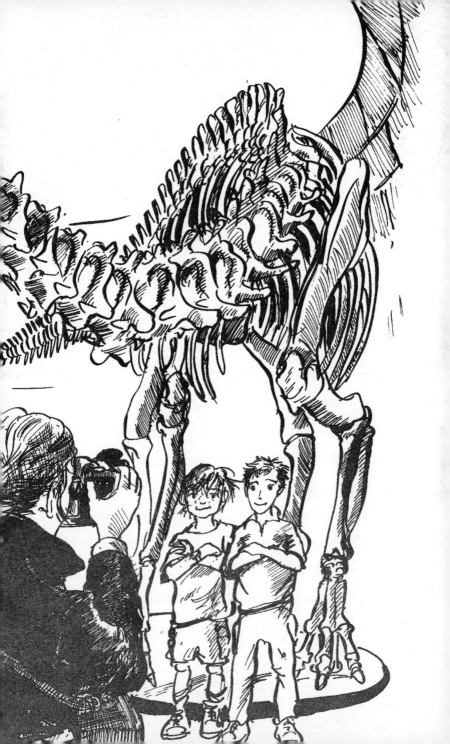

She took picture after picture, then grabbed Jamie's dad and made him pose over by the Cretaceous landscape model.

Tom rubbed his eyes. 'I'm seeing stars after all that!'

'But imagine how many photos she'd take if she saw a real live edmontosaurus,' said Jamie.

'We've never seen a real one close up,' said Tom.

'Maybe we will one day,' Jamie whispered.

Jamie and Tom shared an amazing secret. They had discovered Dino World, a land of living dinosaurs, and they visited it whenever they could.

'I wonder why we haven't already seen one,' said Tom.

'This will tell us where to look,' declared Jamie. He turned on his Fossil Finder and typed in: edmontosaurus.

 170

'*HERBIVORE*,' he read from the screen. '*ATE LEAVES AND BRANCHES. SLOW MOVING. WALKED ON ITS BACK LEGS—* just like our model.'

'But where did it live?' asked Tom.

'It says here it kept to the trees to hide from predators. That was its only defence.'

'That explains why we've never seen one,' said Tom, 'if they were always hiding. That should be our next dinosaur mission—hunt the eddie!'

Jamie put the Fossil Finder away in his backpack. He had a gleam in his eye. 'Maybe I could ask if we can have a break?'

Tom grinned. 'Are you thinking what I'm thinking?'

'Time for a trip to Dino World!'

Dad was being photographed next to the triceratops skull so Jamie and Tom ran up to Grandad. He was frowning at his reflection in a display case.

'Look at me,' he said, before Jamie had a chance to speak. 'Why can't I wear my old jumper and trousers like I do every other day of the year? I feel silly all done up like a dog's dinner.'

'But you look so smart in that suit, Grandad,' said Jamie. 'No one will look at the exhibits. They'll all be admiring you.'

'Get away!' Grandad laughed as he straightened his tie. 'They'll just think I'm another fossil. Now what are you two scamps after? Out with it.'

'It's nothing really,' said Jamie casually. 'It's just that, well, the museum's ready now so we were wondering if we could go outside for a while.'

Grandad looked at the ankylosaurus-shaped clock on the wall, showing nine fifteen. 'Don't see why not,' he said. 'As long as you're back sharp at one for the ceremony—clean and tidy.'

'Thanks, Grandad.' Jamie swung his backpack onto his back and hurried out of the lighthouse, Tom right behind him.

They scrambled across the beach and up to the cave entrance high in the cliffs.

Making sure no one was in sight, they slipped inside. Jamie dug in his backpack for his torch, but his hand closed around something lumpy and hard.

'Hey, look,' Jamie said, pulling it out along with the torch. 'This is the ammonite I found on my first day in Dinosaur Cove.'

'The first day we discovered Dino World,' Tom remembered.

Jamie tossed the fossil in his backpack and shone the torch on the five fossilized footprints in the stone floor. Every time he saw them he felt the same rush of excitement.

'Let's get back there,' he said. The boys trod in each of the dinosaur prints.

One ... two ... three ... four ... FIVE!

 174

The dark cave disappeared and they stepped into the scorching heat and dazzling light of Dino World.

'It's great to be back!' exclaimed Tom, looking at the huge trees and dense jungle undergrowth around them.

Instead of the usual hum of insects and distant calls of dinosaurs there was an eerie silence.

'Listen!' Jamie said.

Tom listened hard. 'I can't hear a thing.'

'Exactly,' said Jamie. 'Something's not right.'

CHAPTER 2

SEARCH:

'Wanna!' called Jamie. His voice sounded strange, echoing through the silent trees. 'Where are you, Wanna?'

There was no sign of the friendly little dinosaur who usually came to greet them. The boys began searching the undergrowth, pushing aside giant tangled creepers.

There was a rustling in a nearby laurel bush. 'What was that?' Jamie stopped. 'Wanna?'

The little wannanosaurus crept out from between the leaves, his eyes darting about nervously. Jamie and Tom rushed over and hugged him.

'You don't know how pleased we are to see you,' said Tom, scratching him hard on his scaly back.

But Wanna just gave a feeble grunk.

Tom frowned. 'This isn't like you, Wanna. What's the matter?'

Jamie reached up into a tree and picked some orange fruit. 'I know what you need, boy,' he said. He tossed one to Wanna and put the others in his backpack.

Wanna looked warily around and then gulped the fruit.

'One thing hasn't changed,' said Jamie. 'Wanna still loves gingkoes.'

'Another thing hasn't changed,' Tom said, holding his nose. 'The gingkoes are still as smelly as ever.'

'But everything else is different.' Jamie frowned. 'Let's find out what's going on.'

With Wanna sticking close to their heels, they made their way through the jungle to a gap in the trees where they could look out over the Great Plains. The plains lay below them, shimmering in the heat—completely deserted.

'There should be herds of triceratops and

hadrosaurs and loads more,' said Tom in disbelief. 'I don't like it.' He pulled out his binoculars and scanned the plains. 'There's nothing moving at all, except the geyser spouts of course. They're still shooting up into the air.'

'What if the dinosaurs are gone?' whispered Jamie.

Tom looked at him, horrified. 'No, they must be here somewhere.'

The boys started down the steep slope of Gingko Hill, but Wanna hung back, trembling and grunking anxiously.

'Come on, boy,' called Jamie, holding out a gingko from his bag.

The little dinosaur crept forward and ate the fruit. He didn't leave their side as they trampled through the hot, damp under-growth, and jumped the stepping stones over the river.

'This silence is really strange,' said Jamie in a low voice.

'And I've never seen Wanna like this before,' said Tom. 'Not even when we met the T-Rex!'

Suddenly, there was a deafening crash overhead.

BANG!

The boys ducked instinctively.

BANG! Another one. The boys
dived to the ground, covering their heads

with their hands. Wanna disappeared under
a cluster of spiky flowers.

Jamie raised his head. 'There's no way that
was a dinosaur!' he whispered. 'Not even a
T-Rex could make that much noise.'

'So what could it be?' Tom asked.

Jamie and Tom scrambled to their feet. 'We've got to find out what that was,' muttered Jamie. 'Here, Wanna!'

A terrified Wanna crept out from the leaves of his hiding place. The three friends walked through the last few trees and out onto the plains.

'Look at that!' gasped Tom.

Two blinding lights, as bright as the sun, were scorching through the sky over the Far Away Mountains.

'Meteors!' gasped Jamie, screening his eyes from the glare.

The boys watched as the glowing objects shot towards the middle of the plains like supersonic jets. They left long dazzling trails behind them.

'They're falling to earth!' yelled Jamie. 'And fast.'

'They're going to hit the plains,' shouted Tom.

BOOM! BOOM!

There was a
dreadful noise like
cannon fire. The ground
shook and the boys and
Wanna were knocked off
their feet.

The trees behind them
shuddered wildly. All at once the
sky was full of pterosaurs screeching
and squawking, and there were calls
from the jungle—deep and
rumbling. Out on the plains, two
columns of dust billowed into
the air where the
meteors had hit.

Jamie and Tom
sat up. Wanna was
still lying on his back,
shaking.

'Cool!' said Jamie.
'We've just seen a meteor strike!'
'And felt it!' said Tom, getting
up and gently pulling Wanna to
his feet. 'No wonder he was so
nervous and all the dinosaurs are
hiding. They must have sensed
the danger.'

The boys scanned the plains from
Fang Rock right round to the cliffs of the
White Ocean. There were still no creatures
to be seen. Even the pterosaurs had
disappeared again.

A look of horror came over Tom's face.
'Don't some people say that it was a meteor

that killed the dinosaurs millions of years ago? Do you think that's going to happen here?'

'No,' said Jamie firmly. 'That one was so huge that it created a massive dust cloud and blocked out the sun. These haven't. But we can find out more about them.' He pulled out his Fossil Finder and tapped in: *METEOR*. Then he read, '*A LUMP OF ROCK FROM SPACE THAT HITS THE EARTH'S ATMOSPHERE WITH A SONIC BOOM...*'

'That must have been the bangs we heard when we were in the jungle,' nodded Tom.

'*AND STREAKS ACROSS THE SKY WITH A BRIGHT GLOW,*' Jamie continued. '*THE ONES THAT HIT THE EARTH ARE CALLED METEORITES.* Look: here are some awesome pictures.'

He showed Tom.

'Wow!' Tom said. 'We could actually see real meteorites—just after they've landed!'

189

'I've always wanted to see a space rock,' said Jamie. 'Let's head for those dust clouds.'

The boys left the jungle behind them and set off across the vast, grassy plains. Wanna scampered along, looking happier now.

'They've landed a lot further away than I thought,' said Tom. 'One of the dust clouds is right at the foot of the Far Away Mountains —near that pine forest.'

'Then we'll head for the closer one,' said Jamie, 'near where the geysers are.' He pulled out the map they'd made of Dino World. 'That's where we chased the velociraptor.'

'Well, I hope he's not still lurking around!' Tom checked his compass. 'We should head north-west,' he said.

'Shouldn't we be seeing the waterspouts gushing up then?' Jamie shielded his eyes as he peered forward. 'All I can see is steam.'

'The dust must be hiding them,' said Tom.

He held an imaginary microphone.
'And here's Tom Clay taking you on
a quest to find the supersonic
space rocks that have
spooked all the
creatures of
Dino World.'

'I wonder what
Tom Clay has to
say about the
ground ahead.'
Jamie said, pointing.
'It's black!' Tom gasped.
'I mean ... Now we can clearly
see the effects of this meteor strike.
We are entering the blast area now.
All around the vegetation is
singed and ... Wow! I can feel
the heat through my trainers.'

The boys walked gingerly across the blackened earth.

'You're right,' said Jamie. 'It is hot! Look at poor Wanna. He could do with some shoes.'

Their little dino friend was hopping from side to side trying not to get his feet burnt.

'Look!' Tom said, as they came nearer the site of the strike. 'There are little fires all around us.'

Small plants were crackling, sending sparks into the air. A spark landed on a dry bush nearby and it burst into flames.

Wanna skittered off in alarm.

'It's OK, Wanna,' said Tom. 'Stick with us and you'll be fine.'

'The fires will probably have scared off the raptor,' Jamie guessed.

'Good thing for us, because we don't have any bacon to distract it,' Tom said.

The air was becoming very steamy.

'We should have reached the geysers by now,' said Jamie. 'But why can't we hear the water spouting?'

Cautiously
the boys stepped
forward through the steam
and saw a huge, gaping hole.

'This is where the geysers should be,'
Tom said.

They peered over the rim of the pit and
Jamie's feet dislodged stones which
tumbled into the bottomless dark.
They could hear hissing and
rumbling deep
underground.

'It's like being on the edge of a cliff,' breathed Tom. 'The ground's just . . . vanished!'

'The meteorite has destroyed the geysers,' said Jamie in amazement.

'That's some power,' said Tom. 'It must have smashed through the underground caverns where the water heats up. Now the geysers can't spout up any more.'

'The hole looks as wide as a football pitch,' said Jamie. 'And who knows how deep.'

Grunk-shoo!

Wanna was sniffing at the edge, sneezing as the steam went up his nose. There was a sound of shifting stones and the ground beneath his feet began to crumble. Earth spilled down into the darkness.

'Get back, Wanna!' cried Tom in alarm. 'It's not safe.'

But it was too late. With a horrible crack, the edge gave way. Wanna didn't even have time to grunk before he disappeared into the deep, cavernous hole.

'Wanna!' yelled Tom.

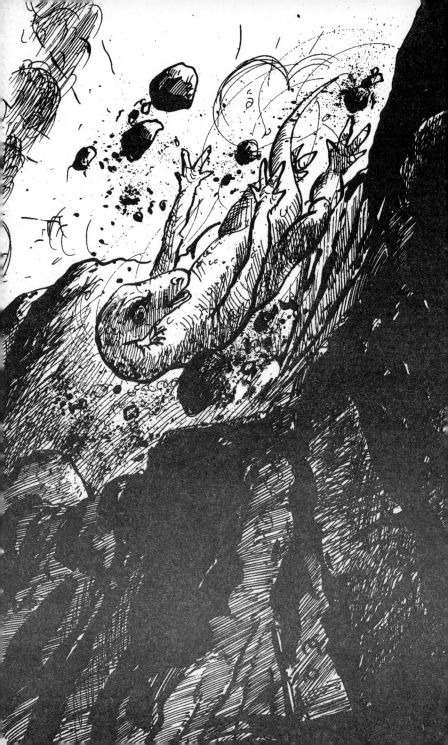

CHAPTER 4

Jamie dropped to his hands and knees and edged towards the place where Wanna had disappeared. He felt the hot steam on his face as he peered into the blackness. Had they lost their faithful friend?

'Wanna?' Jamie called out tentatively into the dark chasm.

Grunk. The response was soft and frightened, but relief flooded through Jamie. Wanna was still alive!

'I can see him!' Jamie yelled. 'He's stuck on a sort of rock shelf.'

'We've got to rescue him!' Tom exclaimed. Jamie took off his backpack and lay down on his stomach. 'I'll try to reach him.'

Tom held his friend's ankles as Jamie leaned carefully over the hole. Through the steam Jamie could just see Wanna, cowering on the ledge, his eyes wide and terrified. Beyond him was nothing but the dark of the deep, steaming pit.

Quick as lightning, Jamie made a grab for him. His fingers closed around one front leg. 'Got him!'

He felt Tom pulling hard on his ankles and Jamie clung to Wanna with all his strength. Wanna scrabbled on the side of the rock wall, trying to help. Slowly and surely Jamie and Tom hauled Wanna up out of the pit. At last, the three of them lay sprawled on the ground.

'That was close,' Tom said.

The little dinosaur darted between his rescuers, licking their faces.

'I think he's saying thank you.' Jamie grinned.

Grunk, grunk!

Wanna seemed to agree.

'We're not going to find any meteorites in that steam hole,' said Tom. 'Let's check out the other landing site.' He pointed to the dust cloud which was still hovering over the trees

at the foot of the Far Away Mountains.

'We haven't been that way before,' said Jamie. 'We'll be able to add what we find to the map.'

'Good idea,' said Tom, checking his compass. 'We're heading north of the geysers, or what's left of them.'

Skirting carefully round the huge pit, the boys set off with Wanna, heading straight towards the Far Away Mountains. As they got closer, the ground around became rougher. They had to step over mossy rocks to reach the blackened earth of the second strike. More plants were crackling around them and they could see that the trees nestling at the foot of the mountains had been scorched by the blast.

There were small fires burning amongst the broken branches.

'On with our mission,' said Jamie. 'Meteorite, here we come.'

'There's the crater,' said Tom. He pointed to a dip in the ground about twenty metres ahead.

'Yay!' Jamie hurried towards it. It was a perfect saucer shape. In the centre lay a jagged black rock, glinting in the sun.

Jamie punched the air. 'It's the meteorite!'

They slid down the gentle slope to the gleaming space rock.

'Awesome!' Tom cheered.

Jamie gingerly reached out a finger to touch the surface. 'It's cold!' he said in surprise. He flicked open the Fossil Finder. 'METEORITES,' he read. 'FRAGMENTS OF ROCK THAT FALL TO EARTH FROM SPACE. THEY CAN MEASURE FROM A GRAIN OF SAND UP TO A FOOTBALL FIELD.'

'Wow!' gasped Tom. 'I'm glad this one's not as big as that!' He tried to lift it but it didn't budge. 'It's amazing that it's cold when everything else around here is scorched.'

Jamie scanned his Fossil Finder. 'It says the meteor is only hot when it enters the

atmosphere and will have cooled down by the time it reaches the ground. The fires around are caused by the impact when it hits.'

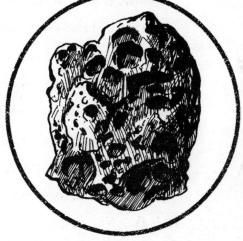

They examined the rock closely. 'It's got shiny pieces of metal in it,' said Tom, running his hand over it. 'And holes like space worms have burrowed through it.'

'Just think,' said Jamie, jumping on top of the rock. 'Less than an hour ago this was hurtling through the galaxy!'

Tom joined him. 'Here's Tom Clay and Jamie Morgan, famous explorers, whizzing past the stars on their own personal meteor.'

'Whoa! There goes Mars!'

'Mind the Moon!'

'Here comes Planet Earth. Crash!'

Jamie jumped off the meteorite and threw himself onto the dusty floor of the crater. Wanna grunked round him, enjoying the fun.

'I'm off to Saturn!' Tom announced from the meteorite. 'Hang on, what's that?' he said seriously, balancing on tiptoe. 'I can see a dinosaur!' He asked Jamie to pass up the binoculars and then peered towards the distant trees which were still smouldering from the meteor strike.

Jamie climbed up beside him. 'What is it?'

Tom handed him the binoculars.

'Take a look.'

Jamie aimed them at the trees. 'Wow!' He focused on a flat, wide dinosaur head with a beak-shaped snout and let out a low whistle. 'It's an edmontosaurus—a real live one!'

CHAPTER 5

SEARCH:

Jamie scrambled out of the crater and swept the binoculars along the line of pine trees. 'There's a whole herd of edmontosaurs!' he exclaimed. 'They're massive!'

'Cool,' Tom said, hurrying to join him.

The great lumbering dinosaurs were huddled together at the edge of the forest. They took nervous steps on their hind legs towards the smouldering trees and then skittered back in alarm.

'But they don't belong in the open.'
Tom looked worried. 'That forest must be
their home.'

'Looks like they're too scared to go back
in,' said Jamie. 'Some of those branches are
still on fire.'

He trained the binoculars on an
edmontosaurus at the edge of the group and
chuckled. 'I think that one's posing for us!'

The eddie lifted its head up and sniffed the
air. It opened its mouth, showing rows and
rows of flat teeth.

'Those gnashers would make short work of a tree branch,' Jamie murmured. 'Dad told me they could have up to a thousand teeth!'

'I wouldn't like to be a dino dentist.' Tom laughed. 'You'd need a drill the size of a cricket bat.'

'And buckets of mouthwash.'

'And half your patients would want to eat you!'

'I wish we could get a bit closer,' said Jamie. 'Have we got time?'

Tom looked at his watch. 'Not really. We'd better go. We'll be in big trouble if we're late back for the Grand Opening. Come on, Wanna.'

They began the long walk back towards the geyser crater and the jungle beyond.

'I wish we could tell Dad that we've

seen some real edmontosaurs,' sighed Jamie.
He turned to get one last look at the eddies
and stopped dead.

'Oh no!' he said. 'Look at the flames!
The whole forest is alight now!'

Fierce flickers of fire were shooting up into
the sky from the treetops.

'The eddies don't like it,' said Tom, 'and I
don't blame them. Their home's burning.'

The dinosaurs were backing off from the
trees, buffeting each other in their fear.
The boys could hear their deep anxious calls.

Suddenly a flaming tree
trunk crashed down, hitting the ground in a
shower of sparks.

With a terrified bellow, the herd reared
away and began to run from the burning trees.
Soon the run became a charge. The ground
churned under their pounding feet and dust
flew up round them.

'They're stampeding,' yelled Tom. 'And
they're heading right for us.'

'We better get out of the way, and fast,'
Jamie said. 'Come on, Wanna!'

The boys and their dinosaur friend
sprinted at full speed back the way they had
come, trying to put some distance between
them and the frightened dinosaurs. Soon they

had to dodge the small
fires that still burned here and there
in the blast area from the first meteorite.

Jamie turned to see that the eddies were
still stampeding towards them. 'Wait a minute!'
he shouted. 'If the eddies keep running this
way, they'll fall into the geyser pit.'

Tom slowed down, panting. 'We can't let
that happen!'

'We've got to stop them or turn them away
somehow,' said Jamie.

'We could wave our T-shirts at them,' Tom
suggested.

'Too small,' answered Jamie.

'But we haven't got anything else,' Tom said, worried.

'Yes, we have,' said Jamie, running over to a burning bush. 'We'll use fire. That's what scared them into stampeding in the first place. We'll stand in front of the pit and wave burning branches.'

'Brilliant!' said Tom. 'Let's do it.'

Wanna butted their legs as if to keep them away from the danger.

'No, Wanna,' said Jamie. 'We've got to do this.' He broke off two crackling branches and held them high. Wanna backed away, grunking in alarm. 'Sorry, little friend,' he said soothingly, 'but it's up to us to save the eddies.'

The boys rushed over to the pit, then turned and faced the oncoming charge.

Jamie could feel sparks from the burning branches stinging his arms but he wasn't going to give up. The terrified edmontosaurs were thundering towards them, churning up the dust.

The drumming of giant hooves was making the ground shudder. Jamie looked over his shoulder to see a large crack appear near his feet.

CRASH!

A great chunk of earth disappeared into the darkness. Now the edge of the pit was right behind them. If the crack got any wider, the boys would fall into the pit themselves.

'The eddies have to stop!' shouted Jamie desperately. 'It's their only chance—and ours!'

CHAPTER 6

Jamie and Tom waved the burning branches
as hard as they could.

But the edmontosaurs were surging on,
pounding away on all fours. They were so
close the boys could see their eyes, wide with
fear, and their nostrils flaring in panic.

'It's not working,' cried Tom.

'We can't give up!' Jamie shouted.

The stampeding herd was only metres
away now. Was it too late? Were they all
going to plunge into the crater?

'STOP!' Jamie and Tom bellowed desperately.

At the last minute, the eddies seemed to notice the fire. The leading dinosaurs reared up in terror and swerved away from the geyser pit. The rest of the herd followed, thundering past, throwing dust into the boys' faces.

'We saved them!' yelled Tom.

Grunk, grunk! Wanna appeared and scampered over.

'I agree, Wanna,' Jamie said. 'That was a close shave.'

'Those eddies used all four legs to gallop,' said Tom. 'No wonder they got up such a speed.'

'That's what we'd better do,' said Jamie, looking at his watch, 'if we're going to be in time for the Grand Opening.'

They hurried back towards the jungle. Wanna was his old self, scurrying between

222

them, running ahead and grunking happily
all the time.

'At least we got to see a real meteorite,'
said Jamie. 'And you got your wish, Tom.'

'What was that?' Tom was puzzled.

'You wanted to see an edmontosaurus close
up, remember?'

'I didn't mean that close!' Tom grinned.

They climbed back up Gingko Hill.
Wanna waggled his tail in delight as
they went.

'He knows there'll be a nice treat
waiting for him,' Tom added.

When they reached the cave, they took
one more look out over Dino World. A herd
of triceratops was grazing by the lagoon and
hadrosaurs were plodding down to the river
by Fang Rock. Pterosaurs lazily circled in the
air. They all seemed to know that the danger
was over.

'We mustn't forget to change our map
when we get back,' said Tom. 'The geysers
have gone and there's that new crater. And
the eddies' trees, of course.'

Jamie took the binoculars and focused on the eddies' trees which were still burning. 'I hope the fire doesn't spread or we'll be making even more changes.'

'I don't think it will,' said Tom. 'Look.' Away in the distance storm clouds were gathering over the mountains. 'The rain will soon put the fire out.'

The boys hurried into the cave and Wanna followed.

Grunk, grunk! Wanna stared at them sadly for a moment as if he didn't want them to go.

'Don't worry, Wanna,' Tom said, patting him on his hard head. 'We'll be back soon.'

Jamie gave him the last of the gingkoes and Wanna cheered up, gobbling up the treats. Jamie and Tom waved goodbye and stepped backwards into the dinosaur footprints and found themselves back in Dinosaur Cove. They scrambled down to the beach.

Then Tom stopped. 'We can't go to the Grand Opening like this. We're filthy.'

'You're right. Grandad will have a fit,' said Jamie, 'and I don't know what Dad will do—explode probably.'

'Quick,' said Tom. 'We'll have a wash in the sea.'

They hurriedly scrubbed the grime off their arms, legs, and faces and made a dash for the lighthouse. The distant church clock was striking one.

It looked as if the whole village had come to the Grand Opening, and crowds of tourists too. A queue stretched away down the path.

'Our clothes will have to do,' muttered Jamie as they made their way past the line of people. 'We've got no more time. Hopefully everyone will be too busy looking at the museum to notice.'

Then they heard a loud voice. 'That edmontosaurus would be an easy target!' A boy of about fifteen was looking at a poster for the museum, showing the eddie model. He seemed to be telling his friend all about dinosaurs. 'They were slow plodders, believe me. Anything could eat them if they wanted. Bet they couldn't run.'

'Are you sure?' his friend asked.

'Of course I'm sure,' said the boy. 'I know everything there is to know about dinosaurs.'

Tom looked at Jamie. 'You tell him,' he whispered.

'Excuse me,' said Jamie politely. 'But the edmontosaurus could get up quite a speed by running on all four legs. It wasn't always an easy target.'

'How do you know?' demanded the boy.

'I've seen—' Jamie stopped himself and quickly recovered. 'I've seen the edmontosaurus skeleton inside. Have a look when you go in. Its front limbs were definitely long enough to run on.'

The boy stared at him open-mouthed.

Tom and Jamie saw Grandad waving them over. They marched up to the front of the queue and up onto the little stage to stand with Jamie's dad.

'Welcome to the Dinosaur Cove Museum,' Mr Morgan began. 'The most magical dinosaur place in the whole world . . . '

Jamie smiled a huge smile. He was proud of his dad's new museum but nothing compared to Dino World.

'The second most magical place,' Jamie whispered to Tom.

DINOSAUR WORLD

----- BOYS' ROUTE

Jungle

Misty Lagoon

White Ocean

232

Far Away Mountains

Crashing
Rock
Falls

Great Plains   Fang
Rock

Gingko
Hill

233

GLOSSARY

Ammonite (am-on-ite) – an extinct animal with octopus-like legs and often a spiral-shaped shell that lived in the ocean.

Edmontosaurus (ed-mon-tow-sor-us) – a plant-eating, usually slow-moving dinosaur that walked on its back two legs. Named after the place it was discovered in southern Alberta, Canada, once called 'Lower Edmonton'.

Geyser (gee-ser) – a hot spring, heated by volcanic activity below the earth's surface, that erupts in a tall stream of hot water and steam, sometimes on a regular schedule.

Gingko (gink-oh) – a tree native to China called a 'living fossil' because fossils of it have been found dating back millions of years, yet they are still around today. Also known as the stink bomb tree because of its smelly apricot-like fruit.

Hadrosaur (had-ro-sor) – a duck-billed dinosaur. This plant eater had a toothless beak but hundreds of teeth in their cheeks.

Meteor (meet-e-or) – matter from outer space that glows when falling through the earth's atmosphere.

Meteorite (meet-e-or-ite) – a meteor that lands on the earth's surface.

Pterosaur (ter-oh-sor) – a prehistoric flying reptile. Its wings were leathery and light and some of these 'winged lizards' had fur on their bodies and bony crests on their heads.

Triceratops (T-tops) (try-serra-tops) – a three-horned, plant-eating dinosaur which looks like a rhinoceros.

Wannanosaurus (wah-nan-oh-sor-us) – a dinosaur that only ate plants and used its hard, flat skull to defend itself. Named after the place it was discovered: Wannano in China.

Look out for more
DINOSAUR COVE
adventures...

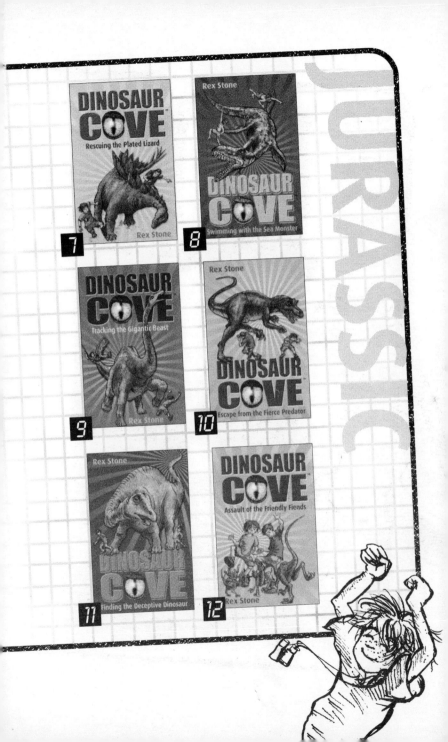

7 DINOSAUR COVE: Rescuing the Plated Lizard — Rex Stone

8 Rex Stone — DINOSAUR COVE: Swimming with the Sea Monster

9 DINOSAUR COVE: Tracking the Gigantic Beast — Rex Stone

10 Rex Stone — DINOSAUR COVE: Escape from the Fierce Predator

11 Rex Stone — DINOSAUR COVE: Finding the Deceptive Dinosaur

12 DINOSAUR COVE: Assault of the Friendly Fiends — Rex Stone